MAR    2008

# THE CHILD

ALSO BY
**Sarah Schulman**

**Novels**
*The Sophie Horowitz Story*
*Girls, Visions, and Everything*
*After Delores*
*People In Trouble*
*Empathy*
*Rat Bohemia*
*Shimmer*

**Nonfiction**
*My American History: Gay and Lesbian Life*
*During the Reagan/Bush Years*
*Stagestruck: Theater, AIDS, and the Marketing of*
*Gay America*

**Plays**
*Carson McCullers*
*Manic Flight Reaction*
*Enemies, A Love Story* (adapted from Isaac Bashevis Singer)

A NOVEL

# THE CHILD

## SARAH SCHULMAN

CARROLL & GRAF PUBLISHERS
NEW YORK

THE CHILD

Carroll & Graf Publishers
An Imprint of Avalon Publishing Group, Inc.
245 West 17th Street, 11th Floor
New York, NY 10011

AVALON
publishing group incorporated

First Carroll & Graf edition 2007

ISBN-13: 978-0-78671-866-5
ISBN-10: 0-7867-1866-8

9 8 7 6 5 4 3 2 1

Interior Design by Ivelisse Robles Marrero

Printed in the United States of America
Distributed by Publishers Group West

*For My Niece and My Nephew*
*and Carrie Elisabeth Moyer*

**1999**

# 1

Thirty-seven years ago, it was 1962. A city bus on a wet afternoon.

The familiar aroma of used gasoline lulled these anxious riders into rest. The stops and starts rocked them—little bundles of privacy looking through dark windows at endlessly familiar, dark, wet streets.

There was a sheen of shadow to that particular sociality, an etiquette for public transport, standing up to give elders a seat.

Anonymous shopping, schlepping. Wet tabloids in weary laps. Here and there a tender mother-daughter conversation. Galoshes.

"Why does that man have no legs?"

"Shhh. Don't point."

Eva's mother's damp, tired burdens. Their bus was inching home now, home to President Kennedy, men in space.

"Mommy, something happened in school."

"What was it? Tell me."

For the rest of her life, Eva's youth would loom before her, retrospectively. Every rainy day would recall these childhood rainy days with her overworked mother on creaky, overcrowded green buses, crawling down their avenue.

"Can you take me there?" (pointing at an ordinary object of international significance like the UN.)

Their conflicts.

A war, several consumer revolutions, and some presidents later, as a seventeen-year-old freethinker, Eva got off the same humbling bus on a similarly rainy Saturday morning to get an IUD. It was the 1970s, the last gasp of consciousness. High school girls were wild horses then—black beauties in pea coats, long straight hair, and looming hips under painters pants. Someone right before them had abolished the dress code. Now those restraints were history, not just forgotten but unimaginable. Sex had become more than an option. It was an obligation and a responsibility. It was who you were. To be a virgin was to not be.

The rain fell into her pockets, flooding the street where the public health clinic sat in a Puerto Rican neighborhood called Chelsea. The girls at school openly told one another about this place, but all went there alone. No boyfriend accompaniment. No chum. It was widely understood to be a solitary endeavor rather than a secret. So white Eva waited on line with Latin guys in frayed army jackets fearful of the clap. Big Afros, they cupped cigarettes in the hallways, acne red from the cold. Transistor radios played. Everyone smoked inside then, ears matching red from another brutal, lonely fall. As required, Eva went while menstruating so that her cervix would be dilated and the Dalkon Shield easier to implant.

"Take out your Tampax and wait for the doctor," the receptionist said, also Puerto Rican. She left Eva in that emblematic cubicle that the sick can never escape and the well only recall on sight.

At that time the clinic seemed worn but never dangerous. It needed paint and was crowded, like the rest of the city. Later, people born in the suburbs would move to Manhattan. There they would re-create the culture of gated communities, trading freedom for security. The social contract would expire, and this clinic's budget would be slashed, its hours reduced. Finally, as gentrification scattered its constituency, the building was closed down entirely and not replaced. The services were never duplicated. The specter of AIDS overrode everyone's anxiety about syphilis. Many former clients died, poised vaguely in someone else's memory. But on that drippy day this future was unpredictable. If Eva had asked the others on line what kind of future they expected, most of her fellow New Yorkers would have predicted *more of the same* or *some improvement.* That about sums up the innocent seventies.

Following instructions, our gal carefully wrapped her Tampax in Kleenex and took out a waterlogged copy of Dostoyevsky's *The Possessed,* required reading for senior English. As the time passed, Eva began to worry that she might start to bleed.

Twenty minutes later the anxiety was unbearable, then finally justified, as the inevitable bleeding did occur—clots falling off the walls of her young, spotless uterus.

Eva knew what was happening to her was wrong; it was a sign of powerlessness. But she did not stand up to it. Instead, she tightened her vaginal muscles, crossed her legs, and wished the blood would sit quietly inside, not seep out onto the white-papered examination table. Fifteen more minutes reading about Nicholas Stavrogin and misguided Russian revolutionaries, and Eva started blotting her vagina with tissues, hoping to absorb the pooling blood. Everything about the situation was undeserved, and yet she went along with it. She knew what would be right, but knowing and doing are two different things. She was afraid of being a problem.

An eternal moment later only one more Kleenex

remained, so she jammed it up there. Fifty-three minutes and finally the white physician got to her now—a bloody, shamed adolescent girl with diminished, bloody thighs.

"Hello, Doctor," she smiled, trying to protect herself.

"Open up." He blandly inserted a metal speculum. "You're crazy to be doing this—it can make you sterile. Okay, relax."

The threat and promise of sterility had long plagued her. Nathalie, Eva's mother, had taken her six-year-old daughter on a tour of infected kindergartners' bedsides to purposefully catch chicken pox *now* instead of *later, during pregnancy.* Deliberate fertility was the Holy Grail, and the pock scar on her forehead, a mark of Nathalie's responsible parenting. The goal of girlhood was to prepare for her future reproductivity.

Eva carried that particular intrauterine device inside her body for three years and then had it removed. Miraculously, no infection, no perforation, no pelvic inflammatory disease, no tragedy ensued. Now the Dalkon Shield is illegal and Eva is forty.

Forty is neither good nor bad, but it is filled with meaning. Again she found herself waiting too long in a suffocating examination room. This one, though, was cleaner, pinker, and more metallic, more expensive. Now more vulnerable in so many ways, Eva waited, dreading the common dread of the dreary institutional demise that accompanies disease. The only thing she found attractive about those four walls was their unfamiliarity.

*Let it stay that way.*

She feared moving into that life, inhabiting forever the boring aesthetic that assaults the dying. Dying would be bad enough on its own without all of that ugly wallpaper.

Forty-year-old Eva's shirt was off, her paper vest draped like a napkin over an elephant. She sat on the table debating a six-month-old issue of *House Beautiful* that lay torn on the mouse-gray carpeting. Perhaps technically she was still fertile. But her mind was not reproductive. Her hips hurt and she feared the physical pain, the financial deprivation, the daily revelation of potential children's unfolding loneliness. She was just beginning to admit her suspicions of children, watching them more closely on the street. The struggle to love justice was so hard in this era, the barriers so intense. Why have children, who could grow up to hurt others or simply stand by and let it happen?

Of course she'd considered it. That deliberation was part of citizenship.

To have children included an obligation to purchase terrible products that alter the soul. There were more of these objects than she even knew: toys with soundtracks that would never be quiet, vulnerable sons and daughters glued to hypnotic machines and then carrying miniature ones in their little palms while crossing the street. But without these possessions her child might suffer and feel inadequate. Which death is better? Nowadays anything eccentric is wrong—there is no social space for singularity. How could Eva impose the pain of individuality on children she adores? And yet what is the point of creating more conformity that will eventually turn on her, even in her own house? If they get rid of rent stabilization, will she even have a house? Can children be raised to be better than their historic moment? Not in this historic moment. Hence, no children.

So many years later and the receptionist at the front desk was still Puerto Rican, but so, too, was the female lab technician, as newly stipulated by law. One of the victories of subsequent feminism. There now had to be a woman in the room so that the male doctor could not molest unnoticed.

"Good morning, my name is Alicia and I am . . ."

"Alicia," Eva delighted, revived by a frisson of justice. "You look great."

"Oh, hi. How weird."

"It's okay." Eva's heart filled with sunshine. This was how it was supposed to go—goodwill and its deserved reward. "I helped you fight your landlord and now you're helping me. It's great. How's your family?"

"My boyfriend's okay and my son is doing very well. He's in third grade. Do you have a lump?"

Yay, old-fashioned New Yorkers. Finding strength in the casual. Worshipping at the altar of the matter-of-fact reality that we live in front of each other, so there is no reason to hide.

"I think I have a little thickening, some kind of mass in my breast. My lover found it. I never would have found it. Did your landlord sell the building?"

Alicia wrote down *thickening* and was *whatever* about the lover. Eva felt glad that she trusted her. More mutual-aid-society citizenship.

"Yeah, now we got a management company. It's okay. I just started here a week ago. Medical technician. I like it."

"Do you like it?"

"Yeah. That data entry was getting tired."

"You get benefits?" Eva asked. That's what New Yorkers discussed these days instead of talking about the weather. It was native cosmopolitan dialect of the urban indigenous in an era where unions and their health plans were something belonging to lucky grandparents or elderly neighbors who happened to come to this country at the right time.

"A lot. Too bad that law clinic closed. It was a good place."

Back to the truth. Forget about thickening breasts; this was the real danger. Eva hadn't fought hard enough and she knew it. Every day brought a realization of one more thing she should have done to keep it open. "Yes," Eva mumbled, ashamed.

"That's a shame." Alicia nodded. They both knew.

The door opened just then and an older man walked in, thinking deeply about something else.

"Hello, I'm Dr. Pollack. This is Alicia."

*Oh no,* Eva worried. *He thinks nothing happens in a room before he comes into it. Bad sign.*

"Let's see what you've got here."

Dr. Pollack handed her X-rays over to Alicia, who

placed them on the light wall. Eva could tell that he was a somewhat religious Jew, despite lack of head covering. It was the way he didn't look at her, and that timbre of speech—quick, deliberate, profoundly questioning within a very rigid framework. He was exactly the kind of person that Eva did not trust.

There were, after all, good Jews and bad Jews. It had always been that way. Roy Cohn was bad, Ethel Rosenberg was good. Henry Kissinger and Ed Koch were bad. Noam Chomsky and Amy Goodman were good. Hannah Ahrendt? Excellent. Ariel Sharon? Terrible. This would always be. Unions were good, and landlords were bad. Groucho was good. Lenny Bruce, good. Philip Roth started out good but ended up self-absorbed and crotchety. Jews who believed in a Zionist destiny and biblical right to the land of Israel? Bad. Jews who hoped that a multicultural, socialist Jewish state could avert inevitable future Holocausts? Well . . . hard to picture. Walter Benjamin? Great. Eva loved him. Emma Goldman? Superb. Andrew Goodman, the murdered freedom rider? A forgotten hero. The Jewish Defense League. The Lubavitchers, the neo-conservatives who opposed affirmative action? All horrible.

On some level it boiled down to religion, didn't it? Did fundamentalists of any stripe have anything good to add really? It was a delusion after all. A hallucination to see oneself as God's chosen. A crackpot wish with terrible consequences. And now this guy, this religious one, had her fate in his hands.

Thirty years before, when most photographs were as black-and-white as the TV, an Israeli cousin had come to visit them in New York. What kind of Jew was this? He wasn't religious and he didn't care about the poor. Was there a third option? This guy wore gold chains and an open shirt and looked like an Italian. He went to singles bars. His main interest was agriculture. He was a racist. A racist.

"The religious? They're worse than the Arabs," he said at his first New York dinner table, a place where no racist word had ever been uttered. "The Arabs, you kill them like flies, but the religious have twelve children. Hey, let's turn on the game."

He watched hockey. Hockey! The emblematic *goyishe* activity. Hit each other with sticks? Jews couldn't even follow the rules.

Young Eva was shocked. Who talks about other people like that? She'd never seen such a thing. It was wrong. Arabs were not flies. She was outraged. Now she was worried about the religious, and about the Israelis. But even with two more hesitations, she wasn't at all alone. Many others felt the same way.

Today, though, sitting in the examination room, everything was different. Her opinions on these ancient subjects were all nostalgic. No one who cared about those precise things back then still cared about them now. The ones who were still alive didn't even remember caring. Caring about these subjects was an old sock. There was no more family. None of the standards of the former

family had any authority now. There was only this religious doctor, and she was at his mercy. The secular liberal
no longer existed. Israel was a nightmare. She had no
family. And here was this Dr. Pollack, not only religious,
but also a male breast doctor.

"Okay, lie down."

"Hello, Doctor."

# 2

David Ziemska, aged thirty-nine, sat in his Westchester living room drinking a Coke. The TV was on, as it always was for every moment of joy or grief, every conversation strained or resolute. The doorbell rang, and so he sloshed through the dirty shag carpeting, glancing back at the television set to catch a last glimpse of the new commercial.

He opened the door to Stew, fifteen, standing on the front step, smiling his adolescent, crooked, acned, thin wisps of a moustache, skinny dishevelment. He was pleased with himself, realizing he'd grow up to be a rake someday, and then settle into a responsible adulthood that was quiet and relaxed with a secret sparkle about his rakish days, the days when he went wild.

"Get in here."

David pulled him across the threshold, annoyed.

"I didn't know you were coming. You could have e-mailed me."

Stew moonwalked on the thick carpeting while David looked down the street and then closed the door. He had to smile at the boy, all comfy now, chin down into the collar of his favorite worn, brown corduroy jacket. A gift from Dave. While rugged, it had a distinctive quality for being so deceptively soft.

"I hitched to Newburgh and got the Greyhound. Then I got out at Port Authority and asked the token lady which subway to take. So I got to the other side of Manhattan, and then I was in Grand Central. There, I talked to the guy at the information booth who told me how to get the Metro-North. I got out at White Plains and I asked the deli guy, and then I asked a lady with her kid and I walked and I found it. I recognized the street."

"Oh God, you talked to the deli guy?"

The new commercial played for the second time as Stew took his little hands out of his jacket pockets and threw them around David's neck. He jumped up in the air with his lithe body until Dave caught him, swinging him in like a sweetheart, and their lips touched. Stew was small, so people often attributed youth to his size. It was the kind of budding containment that seemed ready for transformation at any moment. But actually Stew would never grow to be a large man.

"I love you," Stew said.

"I love you," David said.

Love had come more easily to David these last few years. In his twenties he'd lost the love of his life, Tommy Jackson, to the abyss of alcoholic behavior. Tommy had acted badly, become ashamed, punished David, then become more ashamed and therefore punished David more. For ten years David had not been able to fall in love again. Now he had finally come to love a number of people. When there was something compelling about a man or boy, something endearing about his homosexuality, David found it easy to love him. There were fewer expectations now. Increasingly, he was leaning toward the temporality of happiness, and the memory of it. That was progress. That was it.

As a younger man Dave might have longed for another fellow simply because of some bait—like a glance that revealed knowledge, or a particular gesture associating with a resonant scene in a movie or with Tommy. But these last few years he had successfully taken in the joy of obsession and had eliminated the compulsion for pursuit. The remembrance of male beauty was satisfying in its own right. Predictably, since he had come to that revelation, men and boys fell into his arms with greater tenderness and frequency. He'd learned how to keep his loneliness to himself.

"I had to see you," Stew said.

"I'm glad. I could have picked you up in the city. Hey, Joe," Dave yelled. "Get up. Stew's here."

Joe shuffled down the carpeted stairs still in his pajamas. It was Saturday afternoon and he'd only gotten off the lobster shift at seven.

"Hi, Stew."

Joe came over and gave Stew a kiss on the lips. Then the three of them had their arms around one another, and Joe and David lifted the boy up into the air.

"I've got to get a Coke," Joe said, waking up. "How's school?"

Joe scratched his balls. He could have been handsome with minor effort, but he didn't care at all. Those officially positive attributes, like blue eyes, went unexploited. Joe accepted himself the way he was and attributed that to being from Canada, where people were not as neurotic as New Yorkers about anything.

"Got any new videos?" Stew smiled.

Joe laughed then and stumbled into the kitchen, door swinging behind him. Stew plopped down on the couch and glanced up at Dave coquettishly. Then he folded his jacket, carefully placing it out of the way.

"Flirt," David said, worrying about the danger, but then going forward as he always had. Personally assured of the appropriateness of his desires, he lowered the blinds.

Joe came back with three Cokes and a stack of videos.

"Here's a new one." He handed out the drinks.

"*Manrod in Space*. It's about those Russian cosmonauts that were stuck up in the fucking Mir. Then NASA sends up an American astronaut to rescue them and he's . . ."

"Jeff Stryker?" Stew giggled.

"Jeff Stryker? You've been watching vintage porn."

"He's my favorite star. School sucks. Everyone hates me and I hate them. I want to get out of my house."

Dave had to nip that one in the bud. "If you leave home, you'll be poor forever, right, Joe?" He looked over for some confirmation, but Joe was busy with the remote. "You'll peddle your ass and be totally fucked up." He did not want this kid moving in with them. "You gotta finish. You'll graduate soon." Dave saw the anxiety on the kid's face and decided the message had gotten through. He sat down next to Stew on the couch. Softened. "High school is *their* party. Just get out and never look back."

Watching Stew relax, Dave remembered Tommy Jackson as a young man before he was ravaged by his addictions. Dave remembered a smiling, loving Tommy with the small slope of his back. Then David remembered Tommy at his craziest—how he would never pick up the phone and told the police he was being stalked, just because his friends were worried. How he blamed David for all of his problems. Shame overwhelmed love for Tommy, but not for David. Dave still believed, as he had for so many years, that if Tom would go to a twelve-step program, Dave could forgive him and they could be together again. They could move to South Carolina. Dave would give up everything he knew if he and Tommy could be together again. Joe would understand.

"Not *soon*." Joe snapped open his soda can.

"Huh?"

"Stewie is not graduating *soon*. Three more years, right, guy?"

"Right. Put on the video."

"Okay, okay, Mr. Frisky." Dave was ready for action. "I remember when I was like you. Boner—morning, noon, and night."

"I hated school," Joe said, sitting down on Stew's other side. "Everyone called me a fag. No one would stand up for me. No one. Let me tell you something, Stewie. Fags have to stick together. Never squeal on another fag. Never. I hated those kids, and I still hate every one of them. There is nothing bad enough that could happen to them that would be too bad as far as I am concerned."

"I want to kill them."

"No one is killing anyone, Stew," David said. "Open your Coke."

They sat on the sofa, sipping their Cokes, watching *Manrod in Space*.

"Hey, stallion." Dave rustled Stew's hair. "Look at the gonzo on that one."

"Yeah," Stew said, putting his hand on David's thigh and then on his crotch. Joe put his hand up Stew's shirt and touched his nipples. Dave and Stew kissed. Stew unzipped his own pants, and Joe started sucking him off while Stew kept his hand on Dave's dick. The dialogue from the video was inane.

The phone rang.

"Shit," Dave said.

"Don't stop," Stew said.

Stew was hard again on the train going home, but he also felt squishy and silly. He felt happy. Listening to the low whine of the passengers, he knew that going to David's house by himself, just because he wanted to, was one of the greatest moments of his life. He could get out now whenever he wished. He knew how. Childhood was over and the possibilities engorged him.

It was getting dark and lights were starting to come on in the Westchester towns. He passed house after house with the TV flickering, so boring, just like his own fucking house. He was tired suddenly and a little cold. He wanted to fall asleep and pretended that he lived in one of those houses so that he could roll over into bed. Someday soon he'd have his own place, and then his friends could come over and jerk off, goof around, and make out. The ugly houses were passing. Every single person who lived in them was trapped. He knew it. They all had someone telling them what they could not do. Harping on their flaws. But now he'd figured out how to get away from all of that, all those monsters.

The train passed through Harlem and he saw black people in their apartments watching TV. Then the train got to Grand Central Station and he had a hard time finding the subway. He got a little lost because of all the construction, but Stew didn't mind. Three times he ended up back in the Great Hall of the station, finally staring up at the domed ceiling, the gold stars and planets painted on its slope. It was huge, old, and elegant.

That was another thing he'd understood on the train. The problem with those houses in New Jersey and Westchester was that they were both new and shabby. Here in Grand Central Station he figured out that old and solid was better. It was like a slap, that realization. He woke up panicked. Not only was he free, but he had his own taste. It was a new kind of responsibility to be discerning.

Stew saw an older, sexy guy standing around too, and went over to ask him for directions to the subway, the one to Penn Station so he could walk to Port Authority and then get the Greyhound back upstate. They talked a bit. Then Stew asked him for directions to the men's room. It didn't take more than five minutes of shaking his dick in front of the urinal for the old guy to come in after him and wave his dick around, too. It was a short, thick one. Too short. Stew thought about this guy fucking him and had an image of the top of his butthole plugged up tight, but then miles of empty space where the rest of that guy's dick should have been.

The guy came over and put his hand on Stew's shoulder. It was warm and old and solid.

"I love you," Stew said, without even thinking.

"You're under arrest," the man said, zipping up his pants.

At the stationhouse at Midtown South, there were three cops making cracks all night. After fifteen hours of freezing, starving fear, one cop took Stew's mug shot and fingerprints.

"Your parents are waiting downstairs," the cop said.

"Oh no," Stew finally cried. He wanted to go back to jail.

"Cocksucker," said the cop.

Stew cried.

The cop grinned knowingly. He knew for a fact that this kid's life was over.

# 3

Eva's plan was to lie down on the examination table and offer up her breasts while simultaneously shaking hands with Dr. Pollack, looking him in the eye. Years of yoga made this an option. She wanted to assert herself *and* cooperate. Was this combination possible? If she could stand out in his mind, then—at night—he would lie in bed, suddenly having the revelation about her case that would save her life. She had to catch his attention so that he'd do a good job. If she acted like every other of his many patients, she would be treated like them. And that might not be enough.

This balance was a tricky business.

On the other hand, if Dr. Pollack turned out to be a terrible doctor, one who does a lot of damage, the plan would reverse. She would strive for him to ignore her altogether. Excess complacency was the way to disappear. Then he could not spot her as a moving target for his diabolical ineptitude. Neglect would be the best that she could hope for.

Eva was waiting for a cancer diagnosis that she considered *possible*. However, she also expected to live. If her life was about to change, she knew she had been a good lawyer. But even her career paled in comparison to her two most excellent decisions: (1) Mary; and (2) No children. These were her gifts.

The list of weaknesses was equally obvious. Eva felt she had spent her life not having fought hard enough for . . . whatever, you name it. Reflecting at that moment on forty years of assorted moments, it was clear to her that in sticky situations she'd often glanced longingly toward battle but ultimately gave in. Now, being responsible and aware enough to know she had to strategize her doctor, she wondered if she was going to have to face illness. That is to say, to finally be ready to fully fight for something without restraint. But did it have to be her life?

"Hello, Doctor. My name is Eva."

"My middle daughter's name is Eva. I have six daughters. Let's see what we've got here."

The examination table was pushed up lengthwise against the wall. Before, while she was waiting, that wall had provided comfort for Eva's aching back. But now the positioning became an issue of concern. If the table had been in the middle of the room, Pollack could have examined both breasts by walking around it. But since the examination table was against the wall, he had to sit on it, lean against the length of her body with his body, and reach over her to shift sides. It created a special, extra intimacy.

Eva hoped this was not deliberate. Just bad interior design. Considering her brand-new commitment to the fight, if Dr. Pollack's bad spatial planning was purposeful, so that he could cop a feel, she'd have to do something. Something. But even the idea of raising her voice made her hands clammy. So she tried guilt. Reminding him of his familial obligations. That he was a father, with children, and those children wouldn't want him to do anything creepy.

"No sons?"

"My son is a beach bum. He spends all his time at Rockaway Beach surfing, hanging out with the girls. Weight lifting. Your breasts are very fibrous. I can't see anything on those mammograms. Let's try a sonogram. Alicia, write down *large breasts with significant markings.*"

"What's a sonogram?"

Eva now had more than two upsetting things to think

about, which tended to be her limit. Something was wrong, of that she was sure. A man should not be a breast doctor, and she didn't trust religious Jews. Plus the examination table was in the wrong place. Additionally, she was upset by the word *large*. It was embarrassing. Plus, she might have cancer. Today.

If she had cancer, it was her own fault. She ate too much fat, and didn't do Cardio-Step-Kickboxing, and had cigarettes at certain key moments. Also, there was the environmental pollution that she had never tried to stop, and bad genes she hadn't investigated. But if this guy Pollack was a creep, she should stand up to him. On the other hand, if she was the problem, then everything was fine. This whole situation could potentially be normal if she was simply overreacting. Maybe within the realm of a world in which men were breast doctors, this was all okay. Normal. Maybe she was so out of it that she couldn't recognize normalcy when it slapped her in the face. It was probably Eva's own fault that she was uncomfortable.

"I put this electricity-conducting gel on this tiny machine that fits into the palm of my hand. See?"

Dr. Pollack placed his shiny, lubricated hand on a wired piece of plastic and slid it over her breast.

This was clearly one of those multitudinous moments in which it was better, safer, cleaner, and smarter to conform. Otherwise, being distressed was confusing, and *he* would have the advantage. Eva should just worry about the cancer. She didn't like this man's hands on her, but that's what she got for being such a fuck-up that she could only afford to go to a clinic. Even a clean, expensive one. It had an elite veneer, but still felt like a factory. At this point she should have been far enough along financially to have her own personal breast doctor.

"I pass the machine over the breast and then . . ." He ran his hand over her nipple. " . . . on the video monitor we can see a picture of the inside of your breast . . . He skateboards, too."

The image came up on the screen.

"Does your son have a tattoo?"

She was sweating.

"No, no, no tattoo. Absolutely not," he sputtered. "Never. I hope you don't have a tattoo."

As he moved his hands slowly on and around her breast, she looked at the hairs on his fingers. The doctor smelled of shaving cream. It reminded her of her own weak-willed, creepy, but never sexually inappropriate father—now dead for so many years. Her father was a Nice Guy. He never yelled. He was a nice, sweet man who let her down regularly in a soft, kind, persuasive, loving way. He was overwhelmed with the experience of not being a boy anymore. By the age of ten, Eva realized that her daddy didn't know how to set the table. He didn't know where the fork went. It was an emblematic moment. He died very comfortably. His last words were "What did I do?"

He got away with it.

Eva wanted to cry, so she looked over at the monitor

instead. She and Dr. Pollack watched little cysts come in and out of focus.

"I know," she said. "You can't be buried in a Jewish cemetery if you have a tattoo."

"They made them have tattoos."

"I know about it."

This was the wrong track.

"Look." The doctor picked up a ringing phone. "You're full of cysts. Hello?"

He spoke into the receiver while leaning back against Eva's prone body. His gooey, hairy hand still slid up and down her breast.

"Mrs. Pagano? I'm glad you called. Yes, I'm afraid I have bad news for you. The tumor was malignant."

Dr. Pollack continued to move his hand, cradling the phone on his shoulder, both eyes on the video monitor. Multitasking.

"Yes, Mrs. Pagano, you need to make an appointment for a double mastectomy."

Pollack became slightly absent-minded now, almost glassy-eyed, like he was playing a video game.

"No . . . no . . . no. We won't know until we see the nodes. I am telling you the truth, Mrs. Pagano. We won't know your chances until we see the nodes . . . Mrs. Pagano, there is no need to count on the worst."

He turned toward Eva and raised his eyebrows. Then he went back to the monitor. "Nowadays with radiation, chemo, and meds, you may have a good chance."

Eva felt like a mouse pad. By this point in the

proceedings, she knew it was not only *her* fault that she was uncomfortable. Something was definitely not okay about the way the doctor was handling things.

"Call the surgeon and make an appointment. Who is your surgeon? . . . He's good . . . Yes, I'm telling you the truth. If I knew for certain that you were dying, I would tell you."

She had to get out of there. Eva looked over at Alicia. She was filing, oblivious. Eva stared at the appliqués on Alicia's fake fingernails. So ornamented. Then she imagined her own bare, plain scalp.

Standing up and running away while Dr. Pollack was sitting on her, talking on the phone with his hand running up and down her breast just seemed too hard to do. She eyed her shirt hanging on the door and calculated its distance from her arm. As soon as he hung up the phone she would make a break for it.

"Mrs. Pagano, I know this is quite a shock."

Then, abruptly, Pollack hung up.

"Eva," he said. "We need to aspirate two cysts and do a biopsy."

She felt relief and panic. Relief because Mrs. Pagano was gone, off into her own despair, so Eva had only her personal potential cancer to deal with. The word *biopsy* meant she had to stay put. So she didn't have to be rude, doctorless, earn yet another person's disapproval while her problems stayed unresolved. Eva had been saved from disdain by the threat of death.

"Right now?"

"Yes, a core biopsy."

*He thinks this is all okay,* she gauged. The doctor did not feel guilty about his own behavior. Only *she* felt guilty about hers. He thought he was doing her a favor. Okay, as long as he was sincere, though wrong, she could go along with it.

"Wait," she said. "I have to call my insurance company."

"Okay. There's a pay phone in the waiting room."

"Thank you, Doctor. I need preapproval," she said metaphorically and materially. "Or they won't reimburse."

# 4

All the way home in the car, Stew convulsed in fear. His teeth buckled and his face split. He knew he had told too much to Officer Bart.

*Never squeal on another fag.*

Idiot.

No matter what Stew managed to think up on the spot, Bart always had another question. The guy showed no mercy.

This wasn't like at home, where Stew could just shut down. There, people didn't answer questions, because they didn't want to and that was good enough. No. This cop played a different game. He demanded a reason for everything. There was no slack. *Why were you in Grand Central? Why do you have a used round-trip ticket to White Plains? Who did you go to meet?* This was jail. Stew had to say something.

"Some guys."

As soon as he said it, Stew wanted to kill himself. Idiot. Asshole.

"How many times have you seen these guys before?"

Stew mumbled some number and then couldn't remember what it was. Officer Bart pulled all this stuff trying to find out their names.

Of course, Stew's parents didn't say a word in the car. They weren't like that. Stew hoped they'd just drop it. And they tried to. But then the next morning the whole nightmare started again when Officer Bart came over to their house. Now Stew's parents were embarrassed that they hadn't mentioned any of it and that they hadn't found out anything new. The whole family was being forced by the police department to talk about it and pretend to care. They had to put on a big show for the cop. It was uncomfortable for all of them. The whole Mulcahey family felt guilty, and they wanted every sign of their guilt to go away.

"Officer Bart," Brigid said, frighteningly girlish. "Of course we're very upset by this. We don't know what to do. We don't even know what to feel."

Stew watched his mother pretend to be lost in her own home in fucking Van Buren, fucking New York. That was her trip, and it was embarrassing. She'd ask the other person what they wanted her to feel and then she would mouth it. That's how she got by.

Stew's mother never had a chance. She was brighter than his father but had to pretend she wasn't if she wanted to stay married. That was the big joke in their family.

"I could have made a tough, rich lawyer," she would say regularly.

"Your mother," Stew's father often reminded them. "If things had been different, she would have been a killer lawyer."

Then everyone would laugh. They all knew what a lawyer was; they saw them on TV. Lawyers were ruthless and fucking smart. They win. Real mothers are too smart for their own good. They lose. All of Brigid's instincts went into keeping Stew's dad from feeling surpassed. Marty did not want anyone to be smarter than him, but he wasn't that smart. So the level at which everyone else in the family had to be kept was quite low. This required a lot of maternal regulation.

Officer Bart was waiting. Waiting for someone to talk.

"How should we feel?" Brigid asked him again.

She knew exactly how she'd gotten here, to this very spot. Brigid's parents had a laundry in Newark, New Jersey. She grew up over the store. By the time she got pregnant, it was clear that she couldn't bring up a white child in that neighborhood anymore. So she married Marty. Then her father died without a life insurance policy and her mother had to come live with them. The money situation became desperate. Brigid had to shut up and act stupid so that her mother and her children would have food and a backyard. It was all conscious, these decisions at the core of the Mulcahey family. Conscious and unspoken. That's why nobody talked. Now Brigid's mother was also dead. Carole, her daughter, had her own baby and then got married. Like Brigid, in that order. The only one left in a state of dependency was Stew.

"Brigid." Marty was upset. "I want to get to the fucking bottom of this." That meant she had to think of something.

Stew looked at his father. The guy was a dope and a huge asshole. He was jealous of his own kids. Every time Brigid paid attention to Stewie, Marty would squirm.

"All right, Marty." Brigid tried to lull him. "What should we do, Officer? Is Stew going to have to leave?"

"He can't tell us what to do," Marty said. "We have to figure that out. We've got to weigh the pros and cons." He looked at her hungrily. Waiting for Brigid to do the work.

Despite his wish to appear logical, Marty never made decisions carefully. Actually, he did almost everything on a whim. Every six months or so, he'd knock on Stew's door and demand that they do something fatherly together. But if Stew was the one who brought up the possibility, Marty was too busy. He couldn't take the pressure.

The fact was that Marty's favorite activity was

answering the phone. It could be a sale. Someone might need a swimming pool cleaning system. No matter what was going on in the family, Marty always answered the phone.

"How could you do this to your father?" Brigid yelled, brilliantly shifting the focus off herself. "Didn't you ever think about him?"

"Yeah, I thought about him," Stew stumbled, totally confused. Why did words just come out? What did this have to do with anything? Thinking about his father was a false subject. The real point was that he was being punished but hadn't done anything wrong. His parents should be defending him, like Heidi Fleiss's father and O. J. Simpson's mother. Like every parent on TV whose child had been accused of murder or worse. They all stood behind their child and stuck by them even if they were guilty. Here, Stew had done nothing wrong and his parents were blaming him.

What does *wrong* mean, anyway?

Okay, so there is something wrong with him. Big deal. He's wrong. But even if Stew was totally wrong and never should have been born, he still was born. That's how he looked at it. Doesn't being born count for something? Everyone else around him was doing what their parents wanted: getting blow jobs from girls and getting drunk. He had a secret life. They had a public life. Why was his a secret? Why was he always sneaking around hiding? And why didn't he mind?

Because he was slime, that's why. Only the scum of

the earth likes acting like scum. His parents were right—he didn't deserve to live, but he does live. Now his life would be unbearable. It would be disgusting. Every second of his life would be repulsive. Others would say so.

"But Marty? The officer can make a suggestion, can't he?" Brigid turned back to Officer Bart. "Can't you?"

"Mrs. Mulcahey," the cop jawed. "Stew is only fifteen. He's a minor. In fact, he's a boy. According to the law, he's not responsible for his actions here."

The cop's full name was Kevin Malachi Bart. Stew could tell the guy was an asshole, just like his father. This was another one of those guys who was in charge for no reason other than that they said so, and everyone was expected to go along with it.

"The blame, Mrs. Mulcahey, rests entirely on those two pedophiles. John Doe One and John Doe Two." He glared at Stew.

"Our daughter got pregnant," Marty said, remembering. "But she's a girl and that was bad enough. He married her anyway. You never think some guy is going to get into your son's pants."

Marty picked up the remote and turned on the football game. He couldn't help it. It was automatic. The cop stared. *Was this guy kidding?* Then the phone rang.

"I'll get it," Marty said, happy for the diversion. "Hello? . . . Yeah, we're shipping tomorrow. You should receive the filter at about three p.m. on Wednesday. Always at your service." He hung up.

"Turn off the TV," the cop ordered.

Marty woke up.

"Oh, sorry."

And then there was silence again.

Marty looked around, panicked. He had no idea of what to do. He saw Stew.

"Stew!"

"Yeah?"

"Uhhh. How did you get to Westchester?"

"Bus."

It was the first real question his father had asked him in years. Stew felt like crying. He'd waited so long.

"Good boy." Officer Bart perked up.

The phone rang again.

"I'll get it!" Marty said, delighted. "Hello? . . . Yeah, we're shipping tomorrow. You should receive your pool filter by three p.m. on Wednesday. Always at your service."

Bart took one step closer.

Marty hung up the phone and reached for the remote.

"Marty, don't turn on the TV." Brigid gasped for the cop's benefit.

"I know it's important," he said, waving the white flag. "I just can't believe it."

That was the signal, the change in tone. So Bart moved in for the kill.

"Mr. and Mrs. Mulcahey." Bart tried to look sincere. "Your son is a victim. He was molested. Repeatedly."

"Jesus Christ."

"In fact," Bart said, checking his notebook, "he has

confessed to having been molested on at least three occa-
sions. All of these involved transport of a minor for illegal
sexual purposes. He was molested. This is a clear-cut case
of child abuse here by two twisted predators, who, I assure
you, will be put away for a long time, but only with your
son's cooperation."

"Oh, we're cooperating all right." Marty looked
around to be sure everyone was listening. It wasn't Stew's
fault, the cop had said as much. "Stew, I'm sorry this happened to you. I'd like to hurt those guys. Officer, whatever
it takes to get those guys. How did you meet them?"

"Online."

"Good boy," said Officer Bart.

Stew looked up at the moron cop. He wanted to
shoot a hole through his head. The guy was so ugly. He
had that fake calm that stupid guys with all the power
always have. He was a piece of shit. Stew was a prisoner
of war. This was war. He knew he must never, ever confess, no matter how much they tortured him. That was a
given. Stew had no future—everyone knew it. So what
did he have to gain by squealing? Nothing. At least this
way he'd have honor even if he were dead. If Stew died,
everyone would be happier.

"Why would someone do such a thing?" asked
Brigid. Innocent. This won over Bart. It gave him the
opportunity to have the answer and explain. He loved
that. It's what he lived for.

"I know it's hard to understand. These pedophiles are
sick. They live in their own world, where they try to

figure out how to get into our world and ruin our lives. Otherwise we're strangers. You spend your life taking care of your son. Then one day the pedophiles ruin it. They ruin everything you've done. Encourage your boy to cooperate. Then you will be helping him."

"Okay," Brigid said, showing how profoundly she had been convinced.

"Now, Stew," the cop slurped. "You tell me exactly how these men entrapped you. How they coerced you into meeting them. Tell me everything that they said and did. I've got a piece of paper. I'll take your deposition. You tell me about the first time they molested you. You tell me every detail. I'll write it down. Then you sign it."

"Well," Marty said, on a whim. "That computer is going in the garbage right now."

Marty stood up and walked toward the computer, like John Wayne at the OK Corral. Like he was facing his responsibilities. He stared down at the machine, seized it, and carried it to the trash.

"Don't touch that, you fucker." Stew ran to his computer, sitting stupidly on top of a wire mesh trash basket. "I need that."

"What did you say, you fucking asshole?"

"No, no, don't take it, Daddy."

Marty was livid. In front of a cop! "Sit down or get out! No one is going to fuck around with me. I'm taking this to work tomorrow. Jesus, you're out of control." Job done, he went back to his chair. Now the cop knew that Marty had at least tried something.

Stew gently lifted the computer out of the trash and held it, cradled it. Then he set it back down on top of the desk.

"Well," Brigid laughed, strangely. "That's settled then."

"We'll get over this, Stew." Marty picked up the remote. "Life goes on."

"Actually," Officer Bart said, reminding the Mulcaheys that he was still in the room. "I'm attaching this tracking device to your computer, Stew." He walked over and started twisting wires and adjusting a small box. "The next time those perverts contact you, we'll have their location. You know how regularly they are in touch. So just by looking at the clock, you'll know when we're going to have them. Stew, listen to me. It's inevitable."

Everyone sat quietly while Bart made the attachment. Marty toyed with the remote but didn't press *Power*.

Stew walked over, slowly, to where Bart was working on his computer. He stood next to the sitting cop and was still half the guy's size.

"Is this the tracking device?" Stew asked, reaching for the box.

"That's it."

Stew picked up the box.

"Better not touch that, Stew."

Stew grabbed the box and smashed it down on the table. Then he threw it on the floor and stomped on it until the plastic casing shattered and dug deep into the wood. The whole time he was doing this he was thinking,

*Why? Why is this happening?* But what he said was "You'll never get me."

Bart stood still, letting him tear the box to shreds. Marty and Brigid didn't dare move.

When Stew was finished, he was crying. He was spitting. It was very, very scary for him. What had just happened. "You'll never get me," he screamed again.

"Technically, we already have you," Bart said quietly.

Stew was worried. Why were they all so calm?

"Do what the officer says, Stewie." That was Brigid. She was unusually quiet, like she was telling him something in code. Something so smart it was practically a secret language. He was crying. "You have no choice, Stewie," she said. "He'll arrest you."

"No, he won't." Marty woke up again. Now he was disgusted. This shit had to stop. "What are you, Brigid? Insane? What is this, Stew? This is not the time to be a wiseass. Look, we're on your side, so be on our side. Do what the cop says. Tell the guy what happened. What happened? The guy touched you? Just tell him and no one will ever bring it up again."

"I can't explain it."

"What do you mean, you can't explain it?"

It had been years since Stewie had looked into his father's eyes and seen anything but avoidance. He was overwhelmed by love for his father. He wanted his father to be a father, to do the right thing.

"I'm wrong, Dad."

"Wrong? Do you know how to take care of yourself?

Do you want to be out on the street? I'll show you wrong."

"Marty, we can't send him out on his own."

"Mr. and Mrs. Mulcahey." Bart was tired now. He had other things to do. "I have the arrest report. I know what was going on in that washroom. Stew, you want me to tell your parents exactly what you've been doing? Do you want me to tell your principal and guidance counselor? Do you want this on your transcript? Do you want everyone at school to know? Or do you want to cooperate?"

Marty was pasty. He felt faint. This was too much pressure, too much stress. He wanted to flee, but he just sat there, like he was supposed to. He acted responsibly, like everyone wanted him to.

"Okay," Stew said, trying not to start crying again.

"Good boy." Kevin Bart rustled Stew's hair. It was comforting. "It's the only way out. Now everyone sit down. I've got my pen. You talk and I'll write. Okay, Stew, start from the beginning."

# 5

Eva spent the next purgatorial hour on a pay phone in the clinic's waiting room. Her insurance company's voice mail system was engineered to trigger psychotic episodes. There was no way to speak to a real person. Every avenue led to an endless *Hold*. It gave Eva plenty of time to worry, and plenty of time to look at the other women crying into phones or waiting for their various stages of prognosis. Most of these sister worriers were older. Rarely these days was Eva the youngest person in any room. But this was an exception. Was this to be her future: anxiety dressed as inevitability? After a certain age, of course, no disaster is a complete surprise.

She thought about calling Mary at work, but why make her worry? What good would it do? Mary was afraid of doctors, hospitals, medicine, and the deterioration of the body. Calling would make Mary so worried and upset that she wouldn't be able to word-process efficiently, so she would be trapped inadequately and helplessly at work. Why do that to her? It would help nothing.

Like most of the others in the waiting room, Eva was starting to feel that her situation was hopeless. There was clearly no person at the other end of the phone line. If a real person should ever answer, they would be impatient, mumbling, uninformed, surly, and paid five dollars an hour. The insurance company made clear their contempt by the cold barrage of abusive pop music and repetitious, lying, automated, cheery statements falsely promising that an operator would be with her *shortly*. Who invented voicemail, automatic holds, and mandatory telephonic Muzak? All three were bad ideas.

Eva hung up, defeated, and sat down on the waiting room bench. The men who controlled this insurance company had created a system that was unworkable. She wondered if they did it on purpose.

"Eva?"

She looked, and there, nursing one infant and with

another in her arms, was Adrianna Hopstein, an old friend from college twenty years before.

"Oh my God," Eva exclaimed falsely, as she robotically kvelled over the kids. "Congratulations."

"This is my father," Adrianna said, introducing Eva to an overwhelmed but glowing old man. "Daddy, here. Take Felicity."

Adrianna took out her ponderous breast and fed the other infant as her father held his granddaughter tenderly, bouncing her up and down, creating a false nostalgia for a youthful fatherhood that he had avoided the first time around with job obligations. It was the same breast that Eva had seen at the Michigan Women's Music Festival in 1979, when she and Adrianna and five others shared one tent and ran around naked, smoking pot and blowing their minds. It had been weighty even then.

"How is Louise?" Eva asked. *Could they possibly still be together?*

"She's fine. She had a boy two summers ago. Devon. Now it's my turn. Are you pregnant, too?"

"No, I'm here for a mammogram—I mean a sonogram."

"Oh, I hope everything turns out all right."

Despite the two intervening decades, Adrianna still looked the same. Even as a co-ed she'd been matronly, but now she seemed unchanged and therefore young. She still had that very annoying slow way of speaking, as if her throat was clogged with sludge.

"You know, Louise and I wanted to do something

productive with our relationship, and now we're happy. Daddy, just burp her."

"Still in the East Village?"

"We moved to New Jersey. The schools are better there. Middlesex."

Eva stared at the happy, loving daddy. Was motherhood the only way to get one? Of course it was; she'd already figured that out. Even though her own father was long dead, she knew that producing a child meant she could tell herself it *would* have made him happy, finally. Then she could lament his death, because the inevitable happiness would have given her the father she always craved.

"I've got to go now," Eva said.

"I hope it turns out alright." Adrianna was preoccupied with the suckle.

On the way back into Dr. Pollack's office, Eva remembered when she and Adrianna had been friends. When Adrianna first fell in love with Louise and how horrible her father had been to all of them. Eva had never seen the man before, but she remembered the sorrowful nights over long beers as Adrianna faced his brutal judgment.

"Is Louise your boyfriend or your girlfriend?" he snapped.

That kind of thing was so painful back then. So unexpected and unnecessary. There was no respite from it. It tore young women apart.

Eva had never, ever forgotten that phrase. The cruelty. The wish to wound one's own daughter because she loved. It lingered all those years as a memento of the amazing ease with which people throw things away. She wondered if Adrianna had forgotten all about it.

"What's the matter?" Dr. Pollack asked when she was finally back in his office. "You have bad insurance?"

"Terrible. I have to pay first, and then they decide *if* and *what* they will reimburse."

"What are you, an actress?"

"No, a lawyer."

There it was again. The shame.

"I mean, I *was* a lawyer. I helped people get welfare when there used to be welfare. Now I'm a teacher. I mean, I'm an adjunct. I teach a few courses."

"At a college?"

"Yeah."

Eva had realized over the last few months that if she had fought harder for her clinic, it would not have been defunded. But in this humiliating moment it was thunderbolt true. She had given up too soon. Why did she do that? This wasn't the person she wanted to be.

"And they don't give you health insurance?"

"No, Doctor, I have to buy my own."

"That's terrible," he said.

It *was* terrible, and maybe he was her friend after all. He seemed to understand.

"You see, Eva, between the two mammograms and the sonogram you've had this morning, the cost is already around fifteen hundred dollars."

"I'll have to put it on my credit card," she said. Then she realized that she wanted this man to know how young she was, relatively. "I'm turning forty this year." Too young for breast cancer. She wanted him to care so that he would do a good job. Her breasts and her life were at stake. "My mother had cancer at forty-nine. She survived. How old are you, Doctor?"

"How's your mother?"

"She's okay. Occasionally she gets bad infections from not having enough lymph nodes. But she's okay."

"I'm forty-six," he said. "I'll tell you what." Pollack looked down on her as she was once again lying on that table, shirtless, against the wall. "I won't charge you for the cysts. That'll save about five hundred dollars, although later you'll have to pay three hundred each for the lab. But that's one payment you can put off. I do have to charge you for the biopsy."

"Thank you, Doctor." Eva was ashamed of feeling relieved at having to successfully bargain her health care. "That will make a big difference. It really will."

Losing her job had already taught Eva the essential life lesson that there is a difference between overwhelming debt and even larger overwhelming debt. They all have to be dealt with, but the larger ones take longer.

"Okay." He was excited, happy. "Let's aspirate those cysts before my supervisor comes in and charges you. Alicia, iodine."

Alicia the Silent handed him a dripping Q-tip.

"Okay, here we go." He tapped the iodine twice onto Eva's left breast, the one against the wall. "Kootchie-koo." *Oh God.*

"Look at the screen," Dr. Pollack said. "You can see everything. Alicia, needle! These sonograms are amazing. Mammograms show nothing with large cystic breasts like yours. Okay. Here comes a little prick."

"Oh God," she said.

"Look, you can see it on the screen. Open your eyes. Eva? Eva? Look."

She opened her eyes.

"There's the cyst and there's the needle. There it goes. Watch, watch. I'm right inside you. Perfect entry. Look at all that fluid. The cyst is getting smaller. I'm really sucking you out."

*Help*, she thought. And shut her eyes.

"Amazing. Okay, now out comes the needle. There you go, Eva. Open your eyes. One more time. Okay, here comes a little prick."

Eva was wildly calculating. First of all, she might have cancer like her mother. Otherwise why would they do a biopsy? Second, if she got up and walked out right then, she would still have to pay the fifteen hundred dollars, and the next place she went to would make her pay it all over again. Plus, she would also have to pay the extra five hundred for the cyst aspirations that Dr. Pollack was giving her for free. And as pathetic as it in fact was, she really did not have another sixteen hundred dollars in credit to cover another round. This is the reality of how decisions get made. Even if the insurance company did cover some of these expenses, it would only be in drips and drabs that would take months of phone calls to get a hold of. That was the deal. Five hundred dollars and Pollack got to do his little routine. She just couldn't afford to leave. It would all be over soon.

Once, more than ten years before, Eva's mother, Nathalie, had been in the hospital with a bad infection resulting from her loss of lymph nodes. She'd burned her arm cooking, and the infection spread quickly through all the places where the breast and lymphatic cancer surgeries had removed essential tissue. There was nothing there to hold the poison back. Eva, avoiding her sister, Ethel, and other disapproving relatives, made sure to get to the hospital room when no one else was in the vicinity. It was eerie and smelled of Lysol. Her mother lay on the bed, exhausted. Eva sat on the radiator and watched her sleep. Then, after some time, she watched her come back to life.

"Hi, Mom, it's me, Eva."

"I'm dying," Nathalie said.

It was so strange. There had been times in her life when Nathalie was hysterically mean, but she was never fatalistic. Despite all of her disappointments, angers, and embarrassments, she had never predicted her own demise. Eva, on the other hand, had been in the middle of witnessing the mass death of her generation and so knew, instinctively, that her mother was not dying.

"You are not dying," she said. "You have an infection and you're on IV antibiotics. Soon you'll be better and go home."

"I'm dying," Nathalie said with a rarely exhibited fear.

Eva had to repress a terrible desire to tell her mother

what dying looked like. Why did she repress it? It would have been unfair. After all, this was Nathalie's moment to imagine her own corpse. To replace that, in her mother's mind, with the shocking misfortune of gay people her mother despised would be ungenerous. After all, these men's deaths meant nothing to Nathalie. Nothing at all. It would have been disrespectful. And yet in some ways it could have been construed as a gesture of kindness, a reassurance. Finally, Eva decided to keep her mouth shut. Her mother would not be reassured by the deaths of young homosexuals, because she could not identify with them or extrapolate from them. So Eva said nothing. Nathalie would not learn from her.

Her mother was silent. Eva looked at her familiar face and longed for that old myth she had learned from television—that parents love their children and want to help them. Maybe now, maybe this would be that moment, that chance.

"You're not dying, Mom. I know you feel horrible, and I'm sorry about that. I wish you didn't. But I know that tomorrow you will feel better. You're on IV antibiotics, and by tomorrow the infection will be way down. I know you feel scared, and it's understandable. But Mom, you are not going to die."

"Yes, I am," Nathalie said. "I am dying."

She wasn't kvetching. She was really scared.

"All right," Eva said softly, the way she had always spoken to truly dying people. "I'm sorry, Mom. I wish it weren't true."

Nathalie's eyes were barely open. But it wasn't the exhaustion of the dying—it was the exhaustion of the worried. There, in the precision of detail, is where the truth of life's duration lies.

"I'm dying."

"Okay," Eva said. "I believe you."

"Good."

"Mom, is there anything you want to say to me? Is there anything you want me to know?"

"Eva," Nathalie said, terrified. "The greatest disappointment of my life is that you will never get married and have children."

Of course Nathalie did not die. In fact she had a full recovery and lived to see her other daughter, Ethel, marry a software engineer.

Now, so many years later, back in Dr. Pollack's office, Eva's eyes filled with tears. She was angry. It was an intimate moment of identification with her mother. Facing her mother's cancerous future. Why, in her imagined moment of death, would Nathalie have chosen those words? Nathalie thought she was dying, and that was the message she wanted to leave behind. Why remember that now? If Eva died, her words would be compassionate. Not if, when.

"Now, Eva." Dr. Pollack was still talking. "Out comes the needle. There you go. Open your eyes! See the fluid? Look! Look! It's yellow. That means everything is fine. If it were bloody, then we'd have to worry. What classes do you teach? Law?"

"Freshman Composition."

"You know, Eva. Now that I can see more clearly, I think you don't really need that biopsy after all."

"Really?"

"Why? You want one?"

"No."

She sat up.

"Good. See, I saved you money and you don't need a biopsy. I must be a good doctor."

Eva began to feel sick. Was this all a setup for him to violate her? Did he just say that thing about the biopsy to make her worried and vulnerable so that he could play kootchie-koo? She put on her paper vest. She didn't want to lift her breasts into her bra in front of him. The nakedness was bad enough.

"I'm going to leave now," she said blandly.

"It was a pleasure meeting you. Let me give you my phone number. Alicia, give Eva my home, office, hospital, and cell phone in the car. Call me anytime. Even if you just want to have a cup of coffee."

"Thank you, Doctor." She wanted to vomit.

"Thank you. Alicia, I'll be with Mrs. Alvarez." He closed the door behind him.

"That was weird," she said to Alicia. "Was it?"

"You're probably not used to men touching you."

"Maybe that's it." Eva took her bra down from the hook on the wall.

"He's a doctor," Alicia said with an open heart. "He does it all day long."

# 6

Hockey Notkin had been back in his law office for almost a month, but still no business.

He'd done one stolen pedigree pup.

The owner's cousin had ripped off the Lhasa apso as a cry for help. Hockey talked the cousin out of being so dramatic, then talked his client into not pressing charges, thereby depriving himself of future income. That filled an afternoon.

Clearly the lack of cases was his own fault, but it had nothing to do with laziness. Hockey just could not bring himself to gear up. He knew that "living" meant recommitting to the serious business of competition, but he kept postponing the vow. One morning he even went to Enchantments and bought all the accoutrement necessary for a warrior ritual: sage, weird music, a funny hat, and a white candle. But he never unpacked the paper bag. As the long, empty days stood stagnant before him, it was the desperation of trying to "make it" that he was most loath to revisit.

"Make it?" he said out loud to himself in appropriate public places. *Make what? Make somebody else miserable, that's what.* He knew he wasn't supposed to feel that way. Most people still trying to win pretended it was about making the world a better place, making someone's dreams come true. But Hockey had left that way of thinking forever. He knew now that for one person to win, another had to lose. And since he was going to live, he couldn't afford to lose another thing.

It would be a tough adjustment. Hockey had been out of the achievement system for so long, he'd forgotten how to do it. That last year, the sickest, Hockey had convinced himself that he'd never have the opportunity to compete again. At first, giving up Ambition was a terrible blow, devastating. No mater how ill he became, he could not accept the possibility of life without contest. But then, as he'd slowly made peace with all of his other losses, Hockey began to realize that in fact the competition he had relished and lived for was wrong. As it left him behind, competition became a kind of evil that no longer entranced but instead appeared strangely useless. He didn't just do a snow job on his own diminishing psyche by finding something convenient to believe in. Au contraire, Hockey had actually come to the realization that his new state of consciousness was the *real* truth. Ambition and competition were jokes.

Once, during a particularly long hospitalization, he'd had a roommate, Roberto Juarez, who was seventy-seven years old. The guy was dying naturally.

"The forties are the greatest time in your life," Roberto said feebly. "The fifties are the second best. After that, it's horrible. Call me Bob."

"Nothing good about growing old, huh?" Hockey asked hopefully.

"Well, there is one good thing. But you don't have to be old to get it." Roberto was feeble and spoke slowly, but that was fine, since there was nothing to do and they were both too sick to be bored. "There is this . . . break. This moment where you start stepping out of it."

He was speaking so softly, Hockey knew that what Bob was saying was true. It was movie code. In a courtroom, loud is true. In bed, it has to be soft.

"Out of what?"

"Out of the theater of it."

"The theater of what?"

"Of life." Bob took a rest now.

A few hours later, Hockey asked him again.

SARAH SCHULMAN

"What is the theater of life, Bob?"

"You see the falsity and you feel pity for those who are wasting their energy on it. You know, the game, the silliness."

That hospitalization had been a particularly bitter one. It had pushed Hockey even further on the spiritual conveyor belt toward acceptance of his own death. With this came a new love for other fragile human beings, the ones he had usually run past in the supermarket aisle. That old man in the next bed had finally given Hockey permission to relax. Now he could follow the lead of the dying. It takes one to know one.

But here he was, shockingly back at work, back in shoes. Unexpectedly, Hockey was back in the game, knowing it was a game. This appeared to be a cruel joke of modern medicine and AIDS activism. Hockey had always thought death was the only escape from disease. But things had gone the other way.

He walked over to his office sink and looked in the mirror. He really did seem better. Back at his desk, the sage out of its sack, he lit it and let it smoke. It smelled like an old broom. He watched for a while, couldn't keep it lit. Finally its charred body lay quietly by his side as he turned to the true ritual of sorting out his pills for that afternoon, evening, night, and the next morning. This was something that produced results. He sorted them from the vast array of bottles into his plastic pill container, with its many, many compartments. It was always pill time at the Notkin residence.

Hockey took the big blue ones, three of them, every five hours. He took the big white ones after having eaten fat. The little white ones and the middle-sized red ones were for an hour after eating sugar. The orange capsules were to be taken four times a day, but he had to take the orange pills, four of them, once a day. Swallowing had become a big part of his day.

He put on the funny hat.

Side effects?

These pills destroyed his liver, gave him diarrhea, made his skin break out in horrible rashes, raised his cholesterol, and made him fart. The doctors wanted to take his Hickman catheter out of his chest, but he wasn't ready yet. He needed it. He loved it. It was his connection to life. They opened up his chest and the Hickman let life come back in. He didn't want them to take it away.

Hockey was worried about stepping back into traffic. He had let go of strategy the closer he'd come to death. While sick, his world had become smaller, and aspirations were replaced by the faces of the few remaining friends, their acts of grace. They had fewer expectations and more tolerance, although there were still enough expectations remaining to create real relationships.

Whenever he became greedy in his dying and forgot he was not the only one losing something, his friends got angry and reminded him. Whenever he forgot that a man has responsibility to other people until the moment he is dead, his friends let him have it. But now, as he approached life again, the new boundaries were unexplored. He wondered if his lingering sadness would be considered appropriate, still. Or would it be a tiresome secret he'd have to guiltily keep to himself in order to make room for someone else's emergency? Was the joy of finally living supposed to override all other feelings?

In the old days, when an AIDS diagnosis meant death, as soon as someone actually got sick, many of their friends began to flee. It was inevitable. The friends shook out. Others came in closer. There were always people who were more comfortable with dying friends than with living ones. They preferred the quiet closeness of precious moments to the coexistence that so many relationships are trapped in.

But now that Hockey was better, the most religious bedside relationships became burdened with consequences. Loss was so familiar, for many veterans of the crisis it was the only relationship they could count on. Hockey himself knew the feeling of fearing the living. The living have claws and fangs. They kiss and tell. The dying can't help you get ahead, but they can't stop you anymore, either. They have no currency. The dying can offer the opportunity to exchange little private kindnesses and truths that never leave the hospital room. There is no record, no witness, no backlash.

Sometimes in a hospital bed, or at home, infusing, Hockey wanted to know every detail of the outside world. Who was fucking who. What Carrie Fisher wore. All the internecine warfare. At other times he was so jealous, he wanted no knowledge of it. He wanted the world to end with him. Now, back in the world, he had to be more generous. He had to not want it to end. He had to forget why and how he'd ever felt that way.

Light tap on the glass.

Hockey looked up from his pillbox. It wasn't raining. Someone was knocking on the door.

"Hockey?"

He pressed the buzzer and watched an actual human walk into his life.

"Who is that?"

"Hockey, you know me."

"Is that Thor?"

"You remembered, silly-billy."

Thor entered, smiling, an old man in good shape. He'd done calisthenics every day of his life, and now he was the last surviving authentic leather daddy. Leather skin included. Behind him followed a younger guy, already over the hill. A young, sad man.

"I told you, Joe. Hockey is my pal. He won't let us down."

Thor flipped on the light. That helped. Now Hockey realized why it was getting hard to tell the pills apart. Evening had come.

At sixty, Thor still had that cavalier stride. He still had that shoulder-length blond hair, now obviously dyed, and the telltale thick clone moustache of his notorious youth. He still wore flannel shirts and jeans, the sight of which shook Hockey's memory uncontrollably back to the days he had long put to rest.

There once was a time when Hockey, too, had looked

that way. Everyone they knew had those moustaches back then, those flannel shirts, that rough-and-ready masculinity that did not yet wear spandex bicycle shorts. Thor stood there beaming, the Jolly Green Giant, and Hockey was dizzy with sudden memories of many, many dead faces. Corpses behind moustaches who had died so long ago now. Himself like that so long ago. People whose existence he had obliterated, whose details had fallen off the shelf.

"See, Joe. I told you he would help us."

Joe lingered in the background while the old man went to work. Thor pulled up a chair energetically and then pushed the piles of used newspapers to the floor. He put his jackboots on the desk.

*They still make those,* Hockey thought, glancing down at his own sneakers, the kind he'd gotten used to as the peripheral neuropathy had swelled his feet and legs. Now he wore them out of habit. For a while at least. A little while longer.

"Come here, Joe." Thor pushed old magazines off of the other folding chair. "Have a seat." But Joe just took one baby step away from the wall. He needed it. "Now Hockey," Thor thundered. "How are ya doing?"

"A lot better."

"Good, I'm glad to hear it." He reached over to give Hockey a kiss on the lips. Suddenly Hockey remembered that one time in 1979 when he and Thor had tricked at the baths. He couldn't recall any details, though. Only the long blond hair dripping in the steam.

Joe released a huge sigh, and Hockey remembered the poor guy was still lurking back there, wanting something.

"Joe is in trouble, Hockey, and we've got to help him."

"What's the matter?"

"Tell him, Joe."

"My boyfriend and I got arrested on pedophilia charges."

Hockey looked up. Joe seemed to be a bland man. But then he caught those amazing baby blues. Pale, hand-blown glass. All color, no clarity.

"Dave is a second offender and they've got him locked up, no bail. I got out on fifty thousand dollars. Clean record."

"No," Hockey said.

"Just listen," Thor smiled. "There's an injustice that's been done here."

"The kid is fifteen," Joe said, stepping toward him. Moving in.

Hockey could see it all before him, twirling and twisting in the sea of unpopular causes and gray zones, ambiguous moralities that most people don't want to understand, and essential human contradictions. All he wanted was a couple of condo closings and a few wills. That was enough for him.

"The kid is fifteen," Joe said again. "He's a gay kid. We met on the Internet. No deception. He's been over a few times to have sex, a real frisky guy. The parents are a nightmare, and the kids at school hate him. Now they've got Dave, my boyfriend, in jail on child abuse charges, but the kid is not a child."

Joe was right on the edge of Hockey's desk, looming over him, inevitably.

"Not that that would stop you," Hockey scolded, feebly, while Thor's smile became a reflecting pool.

"Fifteen-year-old boys have the right to get laid," Thor shimmered. "That shouldn't be up to someone's idiot parents and a tight-assed cop."

"I need your help," Joe said.

"I told him what a great lawyer you are." Thor reached out to rub Hockey's neck. It felt really good. "They're going to make scapegoats out of Joe and Dave with everyone going crazy about 'child abuse this' and 'child abuse that.'" He mimicked Joe's Canadian tang. "This is not abuse, and Stew is not a child."

Hockey felt faint. This was going to happen and he couldn't stop it.

"David is facing twenty-five years, Hockey. You've got to help us."

Joe seemed to be a nice guy. He seemed authentically upset.

"Who is going to pay for this?" Hockey knew he was defeated. He was staring at an endless, stigmatized, no-win cause. Another one. Another drain of money and energy with weird, soon-to-be-feuding parties, in an environment of social repression and legal corruption.

"CLACDF."

"What's CLACDF?"

"Committee to Lower the Age of Consent Defense Fund."

Hockey trembled.

"We're not asking for any handouts here. We've got to build a good case and get a good legal team and plan a strategy, right, Hockey? And I have a couple of ideas in that direction."

"No kidding."

Hockey looked over at Joe. Joe didn't have to stand by his lover. He could worm his way out of his unpleasant responsibilities like most people try to do. But he didn't. He had integrity. Hockey could see that Joe was loyal. He was trying to do the right thing. Just the way Hockey had stood up for Jose, and the way Jose would have stood up for Hockey if he had lived.

"What attorney in their right mind would ever take this case?" Hockey whined, letting fate carry him into his own future. Who ever thought there would be a future, and that it would get programmed so passively?

"We don't have one," Thor said. "You have to help us find one. Someone who can make us look good."

"What in the world would ever make you look good?"

"A woman," Thor said.

"A woman?" Hockey rolled it over in his mind, landing on one familiar feminine face. "You're right. That's what we need."

# 7

Mary and Eva were at home on a lazy Sunday morning. The happy hum of a shared life. This is the highest privilege — another person's presence—masquerading falsely as the mundane.

Eva sat on the floor trying to fix her bicycle. Mary was at the computer, both listening to a well-worn copy of *Dusty in Memphis*. The immeasurable pleasure of the morning chat, that constant conversation between two mutually interested people that means true love.

"I don't get it," Eva asked casually. "Why did he turn you down?"

Mary's naturally soft angelic look was so deeply pleasurable to Eva that it transcended everything harsh she might do or say. She was a visceral, visual delight. If the words were painful, Eva could just watch. Many hundreds of mornings Eva looked over at her sleeping lover, her sustained loveliness, and thought, *You are so beautiful, and I love you so much.* Watching her chest rise.

"I've explained this before," Mary said calmly.

"You *have* explained it. But I still don't get it. I thought he loved your play."

Mary was willing to go over this one more time, even though she had long ago come to understand that there were essential facts about her world that Eva could never grok. The Theater was not orderly like the law. Eva was logical to a fault. Since the theater was entirely illogical, Eva would never understand, really, why all that cruel and lovely artifice mattered so very, very much. Why it drove people mad.

"I'll explain it to you again."

"I know you've explained it before—I'm sorry. But I want to get it."

"Okay." Mary was willing.

Repetition had worked in the past. It had taken Eva about three moons of explanations to finally understand that Mary really cared about Christmas and that Eva had to get her a present every year. Then Mary persuaded her that ham sandwiches on white bread with mayonnaise were delicious comfort food and nothing to be made fun of.

Eva had to learn that most people in most places say prayers before eating when they are with their parents. Witnessing it should not be considered an anthropological experience to be relayed to aesthetic friends at dinner parties. Mary spent years convincing her that it is normal to fly an American flag. That Mary's family members are *regular,* not "blue-collar white Protestants," as Eva habitually described them. Just normal. That most people do not think it is "fun" to argue at the dinner table. That when you ask someone where they are from, the typical answer is *Michigan.* Not *The Pale of Settlement.*

Of course, Mary, too, had had to adjust very rapidly to the way Eva saw life. Anyone wanting to make it in New York had to catch on quickly. There was a hysterical kind of ambitious socialist loyalty that Eva, and the other people who dominated New York culture, had in tow. They would wish death on their opponents while inviting gross, dislocated, poor people home for dinner. What was the point? Eva should just take care of her own business and let other people fend for themselves.

Mary could. Mary was robust, she worked three jobs, wrote plays, she did all of this without handouts or scheming. Mary understood Eva's way, but Eva had a hard time figuring out how the other 99 percent lived. After all, Mary realized quickly, her girlfriend was the really provincial one. Eva had never lived anywhere but here. She'd never had any job but lawyer and now teacher.

She'd never had a real job, where it is incredibly boring but you can't do anything about it. And most important, Eva—who had no artistic impulse, and had never even made one drawing in her entire life—Eva had no idea of what the theater world was really like.

"Well, he's one of those producers who wants to know whose play it is."

"But it's yours. Throw me that rag, will you?"

"No, which *character*. They think that a play can only belong to one character. So they walk around saying, 'Whose play is this?'"

"That's dumb."

"Yeah, it is dumb. It's a limited way of looking at what theater can be." Mary got up and poured them both more coffee. Nonfat milk for Eva; she had cystic breasts. Mary, on the other hand, could eat anything. She never gained weight and never got sick. American. Her people settled the West. "But all the guys who run the theaters arbitrarily agreed one day that a commercial play had to be about one character. They don't have enough empathy to care about someone they don't identify with. It's a combination of pathology and privilege. They don't realize that the world belongs to everyone *at the same time*. When you sit on a park bench and look out, the world you observe is not about one person. Life is the protagonist. Human failing. Desire."

"So why does he only want one?" Eva wasn't getting it.

"Because . . ." Mary wanted to be patient. She took out four Mallomars. Eva wouldn't want any. Mary could eat them all. Eva didn't like junk food. She was afraid of it. "He thinks if the audience can't tell from the start who in the play they're supposed to care about the most, they'll get mad. But I don't think that way. I refuse to be back-story, but I know I'm not the only story. Do they?"

That sounded good. She'd made her point clearly—if anyone was smart enough to get it. Mary stuffed a whole cookie into her mouth, thereby freeing her hands for the more pressing task of typing out that phrase on her key-board. She'd savor the next Mallomar. This one had been a martyr to the larger cause.

"I'm totally fucking up this bicycle."

"Lift the chain, Eva. You're gonna get greasy, it's unavoidable. There's no other way to fix it."

"You're always so sure," Eva said admiringly, lifting the chain. She got greasy and fixed the bicycle. "It works. I'm like the audience—I get nervous. I just watch and wait, wondering what I'm supposed to feel, supposed to do."

"But it's your *life*."

"But it feels like it's taking place in their world."

"Eva, art creates worlds." Mary reached for the chocolate milk. "It makes everything possible. If what I'm offering the audience is truly transforming, the rules should not matter."

"Perfect. You were so right. Want to go biking?"

"No way. You almost get killed three times a day on that bike. I can't bicycle in New York City. I'd never sur-vive. Bikes are for the country."

"But, honey," Eva absentmindedly rubbed the grease

all over her clothes, "when are we ever in the country? You just have to watch out for car doors opening."

"I don't want to," Mary said. "I don't want to think about car doors when I'm riding a bike."

"Mary, you're dropping cookie crumbs on your keyboard."

"Oh shit."

"Dreamer." Eva smiled as she went out for a ride. No helmet. Wrong way down a one-way street. Riding on the sidewalk.

Like she had her whole life.

# 8

Daniel Wisotscky, Certified Social Worker, aged sixty-six, had been logged on to his computer for three solid days exploring America Online. He was still angry about having to learn the computer, but the Mulcahey family's case made it finally essential. What Wisotscky found on the Internet shocked him, in spite of forty years as a mental health professional and twenty years as County Family Counselor for Van Buren Township.

The first truly upsetting thing that Wisotscky uncovered was the Hairy Chest Page. This was a site for homosexual men, and, presumably, heterosexual women, with advanced fetish compulsion toward men with hairy chests. Wisotscky had previously been aware of a wide range of sexual fetishes, such as "pregnancy pornography," featuring pregnant models. He'd also discovered online images of naked women shaving their pubic hair and ones of women being rained on. However, there was a strange ironic stance to the Hairy Chest Page that he found particularly grating: it had no shame. It was like making a fetish out of a Bic pen.

Wisotscky found this idea to be terribly disturbing. Not only did the site show full-frontal nudes of hairy men that any child could download, but the designer of the Web page also made available a fifteen-thousand-example annotated listing of all the moments in American and European cinema in which an actor bared a hairy chest. It was insane.

Wisotscky noted that there was a new arrogance behind deviant sexual behavior in the computer age. There was a flagrant ingenuity, almost a smirk. The next site he went to was dominated by the image of a young male child orally sodomizing an adult. It was more old-fashioned and made clear to him that the electronic light field of the computer was hypnotic. This, combined with the easily accessible lurid imagery, could convince any child to participate, unwittingly, in the complex trappings laid by a pederast.

"Mr. Wisotscky, the Mulcaheys are here to see you."

In stumbled a bedraggled working-class couple from the township, their overly seductive adult daughter—typically named Carole—and their alienated, adolescent son. The husband was standard from these parts. Late forties, looked sixty. Never took care of himself. Bad food, bad shampoo. The mother was inappropriately girlish. She was flirtatious and overfeminized in a manner that was unbecoming. Infantilized. The son, predictably sullen, was quite small for his age. The sister was underclad.

"Mr. Mulcahey, Stew." He looked at the chart. "Carole. You're the married sister. Mrs. Mulcahey." Another glance. "Brigid. Please have a seat, all of you. There, on the couch, or I also have these two chairs. Please sit down. Good."

He noted that the boy gave up the best chair to his mother. Good, everything would have a happy ending.

"What else do you know about us?"

"Can I call you Marty? I am Daniel Wisotscky, County Family Counselor for Van Buren Township. I see that you were referred by Officer Bart, that you're trying to make some tough decisions about your family."

"I don't understand why we have to talk to you about our decisions." Marty was putting on a show for his daughter. "It's our family, we'll do what we want."

Wisotscky said nothing, so of course there was an awkward silence. He had long wished for the day when these blue-collar families would come into therapy as naturally as they took their cars in for lube jobs. But, unfortunately, these people would rather buy some self-help book or watch a daytime talk show than put their lives into the trained hands of a professional who could make a difference. It was the submission that was important, the capitulation to experience that signaled a real effort to change. What the alcoholics called "helpless."

"Daddy, there are some problems." There was Carole, being the substitute wife.

"I don't even know this guy."

"I know," she said sweetly. "But the officer said you can't do anything without the approval of a social worker."

"Why should he have all the power?"

Dan smiled at the real wife. "Do you feel this way, Brigid?"

"I have no power over anything, especially my son."

*Okay, so she's the martyr.*

"Have you told him how you feel?"

"It doesn't matter what I say. I ground him, he sneaks out. Do you know what it's like to make dinner for someone who won't look at you?"

"Then my wife and I get into fights."

Carole joined in. "Stew is taking no responsibility."

"I can't manage him," Brigid said. "It's too upsetting for Stew, and it is too upsetting for us."

Stew sat impassively.

"He sits there like a crazy person." Marty gestured toward his son. "He grits his teeth and makes fists. He cries like a baby. He yells at us. He's a bad kid."

"I am not," Stew said. "I just have my own ideas."

"Like what?" His mother sighed. She'd been through that one before.

"Like, Mom—like old is better than like new. Did you know that?"

"Not when you're my age."

Wisotscky noted on his pad that the kid was *inarticulate*.

"See, Doc," the father said, pointing. "What is he talking about?"

"I know he was molested." Mrs. Mulcahey sighed again. "But even before he was molested, he never cooperated."

"This kid has got serious problems that have nothing to do with being molested," Marty explained deeply. He had done a lot of thinking to come to this revelation.

Brigid looked at her husband. "Doctor, Stew is ruining our lives. He is angry all the time. He wants to leave."

"Get it, Doc?"

Wisotscky could see Marty's annoyance at having to re-create and summarize this concept for the doctor's benefit. Obviously Mr. Mulcahey frustrated easily.

"No, I don't," Stew almost cried. "Shut up."

"Doctor," Brigid said. "I'm afraid of him. I'm afraid he's going to hit me."

"Are you talking about your husband or your son?"

Stew laughed.

"Why is he laughing, Doc?" Marty squirmed. "It's not normal." Marty stared at Stew. "What's wrong with you? You think this is a joke?" He pointed at his son and then looked up sideways at Wisotscky for approval. It was like Wisotscky was the daddy, and Marty, the little family tattletale.

Carole put her hand on her father's shoulder. She was behind him one thousand percent. "Go ahead, Daddy. Tell the doctor."

Actually, Wisotscky was not a doctor. He was a certified social worker. But he did not correct Mr. and Mrs. Mulcahey. It made his clients feel more secure in his office if they carried the illusion that he was an MD. Most of the people of Van Buren Township were not aware of the various possibilities within professional categories. Wisotscky softened his face into a more cinematically fatherly disposition. It was what everybody wanted him to be and helped encourage transference.

"Are you feeling depressed, Stew? Tell me, because there are other alternatives."

"He's not the only one." Brigid gave a big gasp now and put her hand on her forehead. To Wisotscky she looked like the Irish washerwomen of his youth back in Ashtabula, Ohio.

"What do you think is the solution? Mr. and Mrs. Mulcahey?"

"Well, we've been talking it over." Marty looked at his wife. "And we think he'd be better off in a juvenile home, some kind of reform school or military camp. Some place where he'd learn a lot of discipline, like I did in the army. I figure after a few weeks of that he'll appreciate us more and will learn how to behave. Nothing permanent, Stewie. Just long enough to help."

Brigid nodded. "We both agree."

"We *all* agree." Carole was the royal guard.

"Stewie." Brigid tried to smile. "It's just temporary. I'm afraid, Doctor, that he won't understand. That he'll grow to resent us."

"Mommy, I resent you already," Carole said. "For not doing anything."

"Shut up." Stew looked at the floor.

Dan leaned toward Brigid compassionately. "Why do you let him talk to you that way?"

"I can't stop him."

"Tell me a little bit about yourself, Mrs. Mulcahey. What do you do for a living?"

"I work at Soto's Insurance."

"Like it?"

"No."

"Have you thought about getting a new job?"

"If I ever lost my job, I'd never find another. Who wants an old hag who doesn't know computers? I hate computers. They've ruined everybody's life."

Stew laughed. "I don't feel sorry for you."

"Well, you should."

"Brigid, why should he feel sorry for you?"

Mr. Mulcahey looked at his son. Wisotscky could tell that the father was nervous. "My wife and I had some problems. But now they're straightened out."

"My father had a girlfriend."

Marty blew up. "You make everybody's life miserable!" He looked around, humiliated. "You think I like sitting here? You think I like taking time off from work? You're like a crazy, sick person. You are the problem. You are wrong, kid. You're a wrong kid. You hear what I'm telling you? I don't know what else to do."

Wisotscky let the requisite moment of silence pass and then did his thing.

"Stew, it sounds like you've made your father pretty angry. Why do you think your father is so angry?"

Stew was so angry he couldn't talk. He pressed his teeth together ferociously in order to keep from saying anything that could be called inappropriate, thereby sealing the lid on the box he was backing into.

Wisotscky noted *repressed rage at father* on his pad.

Stew balled up his fists to keep from crying at his father's comments. His position was untenable. There was a limit, Wisotscky knew, to how much Stew could keep under wraps. Eventually he would spill it. Perhaps a short visit to a juvenile detention facility would do the trick. Those clenched teeth distorted his whole face.

Wisotscky noted *uncontrollable* on his notepad.

"Stew," Brigid said, reaching out for his little shoulder. "How can we help you to behave if you won't say anything? We want it all to work out, but you have to cooperate, too." She took her hand away.

"Why are you lying?"

Brigid was up to her elbows in suds again.

"See, Doctor? I'm in over my head. Marty and I are trying to do everything you people tell us to do, but you're not helping us handle it. Right now, with Stew acting this way, I can't deal with him. If you make me take Stew home, something terrible is going to happen."

"You stop that, Brigid, or I'm out of here," Marty blasted, exhausted. "I can't take any more." Marty looked scared. "Control yourself, Stew."

Wisotscky could see that the mother was narcissistic and childish. She acted like a girl. If the father would give the son some contained attention, everyone would be satisfied. And the father would feel better about himself, more self-esteem.

"I *am* controlled." Stew was enraged. "I'm not doing or saying what I want to say or do. Isn't that what you want?"

"Stew." Wisotscky decided to wrap it up. "Do you want to have a short-term residency in a juvenile detention facility?"

"You've got to stop it, Dad."

"Stop what, Stew? Your father isn't saying anything."

"No, he said it before. He's got to stop all those sentences beginning with the word *you*. I can't take them anymore. Listen to me, Dad. I can't take it. I'm not just saying that. I'm telling you the truth. Please, please stop."

"I'm talking, too," Brigid said.

"Stop what?" Marty said. "What are you talking about? Are you hearing voices?"

"Stop everything that starts with the word *you*. I can't take it, I'm not kidding."

That was it. Marty gave up. Wisotscky saw him get overwhelmed. A little more paternal confidence and everything would be fine here.

"See, Doc, the kid doesn't make any sense. Now he wants to stop me from talking. Well, kid, you can't tell me how to talk. I'm going to tell *you* how to talk. Shut up. That's how you should talk."

"Mr. and Mrs. Mulcahey, Carole, please step outside for a minute. I want to speak with Stew alone."

Wisotscky sat back in his chair, watching, as Brigid, Carole, and Marty obeyed, angrily, awkwardly, silently, negotiating their exits.

# 9

The next day, Monday, Eva came back from work, groceries in hand. And flowers. Something horribly unexpected had happened on the way home. But inside their apartment, Mary was the one waiting for comfort.

"I'm so glad you're here," she said, tiny, vulnerable, relieved.

This sweetness opened Eva's heart. It healed her. She kissed the love of her life.

"So am I."

"I walked into the theater and he said, 'I can get this play done, and I can do it soon.'"

"Wow!" This was *great* news. "The Federal Theater said that!" Eva put down the shopping bags and started jumping around.

"Wait!"

"Oh, okay." Listening quietly, Eva unpacked the vegetables. This was her greatest pleasure. To belong to someone. Someone to come home to, to talk to, someone waiting for her. Someone to listen to. To look at. This was it.

"That's what I thought." Mary was pacing, gesticulating, finally supported enough to be outraged. "I thought, *Wow, this is finally going to happen.*" She lit a cigarette.

The radishes were gorgeous. They were so white, they were like stars. Eva put them on a blue plate. It looked incredibly weird.

"Okay." Mary imitated the gruff, dumb, generically male artistic director. "'But we have to make the play work,' he says. 'It needs one good story.'"

"Okay." Eva was open, wanting to get it. "Oh wait, is this that *whose play is it* thing?"

"Wait!" Mary inhaled.

"Okay."

"'I love the part about the boy,' he says. 'But those two gay women will have to go. They're a distraction from the real story. What in the hell do they have to do with that boy?'"

"I like them," Eva said, offering Mary a radish. "I like those two gay women. "She started putting the flowers in a vase. "Did you explain?"

Yes, Mary had explained. This was her third appointment with the dramaturg at the Federal Theater. The first time, she'd come all dressed up and waited in the lobby for two hours while the seen-it-all tired queen at the switchboard kept ringing his line and getting no answer.

"But he said two o'clock."

"He's up there." The receptionist fluttered, batted his eyelids, drooped his eyelids, raised his eyebrows, fully activated all faggoty gestures that could possibly emerge from the ocular area. "He just don't answer."

The second round was three months later in a snow-storm. She'd braved blocks of no buses, no sidewalks, no paths. Arrived in the stone-cold lobby and waited for two hours. Then braved them all again empty-handed.

This was strike three. The dramaturg was a sort of cruel, sarcastic young man. He had a respected actor for a boyfriend, and that gave him even more status. It made them an "It" couple. And therefore part of the infamous theatrical hierarchy. That was one thing that had taken Mary years to figure out. The Hierarchy. If you were lower than someone, they were dismissive to you, and if you were higher, they were subservient. It had nothing to do with whether or not someone authentically liked her. It had nothing to do with her at all. If one day she could get some currency, then people who had been awful would be nice. And that would feel great—she knew it. But how to get from here to there?

So finally she'd made it into his office, where he sat behind an important desk and she sat in a single chair. But she was ready. She'd come prepared to explain.

"See," Mary told this man with power. "I grew up in a small town called Del Sol, California, where the wind changes direction many times a day. It taught me that in life there is momentum on all paths at once."

He was still breathing.

It was so warm, that wind. It pushed you forward, kissed your soul, stood in your way. One force in many directions, each with its own purpose.

"So the two gay women in my play are actually interesting. But the audience doesn't know how to watch them. They're not used to them. They're used to watching men."

He seemed to still have a pulse.

"That's what I have to offer an audience that's special. The big news that we're all in the same world, together. And that no one needs to see a boy in order to see himself. You know?"

Something was going wrong. Mary started to panic. The man who was supposed to finally help her, the one who was supposed to be different and open the door. That man wasn't coming through. He wasn't getting it.

"You know? The boy and the women are each other's story. One story. The space between their experiences is the story. One story. Like the wind. One wind."

She sat back watching this lump of entitlement decide her fate. She'd brought him a gift, didn't he see that?

He smiled. Good.

"Keep me posted."

Then he got back on the phone.

"I'm going to have a glass of wine."

"No, thanks," Eva said and kissed her on the mouth. "I believe in you."

As soon as she tasted the Chardonnay, Mary started strategizing for her meeting the following day with a really big producer. She had to change her method. Telling the truth did not work. This time, no matter what, she would be what he wanted her to be.

If he's a nice fag, she'll be herself and flirt a little and be smart. If he's an asshole fag, she'll be really competent and smart, no flirting, but she won't be smarter than him. If he's straight, she'll flirt as long as there are no straight women in the room, because they can do it better and she'll look dumb. If there is a straight woman in the room, she'll have to remember not to flirt with her, and not to be smarter than her in front of him. Sisterhood and all that. What if there's a lesbian in the room? There won't be.

"What time are you meeting Hockey?"

"We said he'd come pick me up at seven thirty, so he'll be here at seven." Eva placed the vase of flowers on the table. Then she sat down on the couch. She touched her lover's sloping shoulder with a private gratitude and grace. "What are you going to do?"

"I got a tape of the first five episodes of that new series, *OB/GYN*. I'm gonna watch them, try to figure out the formula."

"Have I ever seen that one?"

"Yeah." Mary was excited. She had her pad and pencil ready. "Remember? The black guy got shot. The white girl got breast cancer and died. The nurse used to be a dominatrix, and the radiologist needed a green card?"

"They're all like that."

"No, no, no. In this one a blind girl was kidnapped, someone stole a Six train, the orderly fell in love with the elevator, and the opera singer got breast cancer and died?"

"Oh, okay . . . Honey," Eva said softly. "Something really creepy happened."

Mary stopped, looked up. She saw the expression on Eva's face.

"What happened?"

"At the Bar Association cocktail party. My sister. It's so ridiculous."

Mary cared. "Of course you're upset."

"Yeah, I'm upset."

"What happened?"

Sometimes love is just asking an open-ended question, then sitting back and listening with compassion. It can be a question like *What happened?* Or it can be something even smaller, like *What is a poem?* Or *What was it like when you were young?* It's the opening of a window, the creation of space. The interest. The time.

"Well," Eva said, now feeling it. Now having her

turn. Now being in her home with her lover, having her moment. "It was bad enough when we found out that she'd had a baby and didn't tell us."

"That was awful."

"But today I actually ran into someone who had been invited to the baby shower. Isn't that bizarre? I had to confess that we didn't know anything about it."

"Your sister, I want to kill her."

"No one's killing anyone." Eva did want to kill her sister, but she would never say so. Mary would say so. Eva depended on her for it.

"Did you finally find out if it's a girl or a boy?"

No, Eva had been too embarrassed to ask.

"Mary, do you think it's child abuse to keep your kids away from their lesbian aunts?"

"Legally? How would I know?"

"Can I go into court and sue for the right to be an aunt?"

"I don't think you can win that way."

All the way home from the cocktail party, she had looked at little children on the street and thought about their phantom niece/nephew. It felt so bad. Eva didn't know how to fight this thing.

"What if I offer to meet our niece/nephew with a chaperone?"

"No." Mary was certain. "Absolutely not. I am not going to let you do that to yourself. This is not your fault."

It felt so good to have someone say *This is not your fault* when in fact it was not. And yet in some way she wished it were, because then she could change it. If the problem was that Eva was an alcoholic, she could go to detox, rehab, endless AA meetings, and many coffee cups later change it all. It would be in her hands. But when the cruelty comes from the outside—in some stark, unwanted reality—she is at its mercy. Unless her sister changed, Eva would be spending the rest of her life following little girls on the street wondering *Is that my niece?* Always longing for justice—to be treated the way that she deserved. To know how to make that real.

"Look," Mary said, refilling her glass. "There are a lot of lost kids around. Remember yourself. What if there was a child who really needed you?"

"If she needed me?"

"Or he?"

"If he needed me?"

"Well, maybe someday our niece/nephew will be that child. But maybe it'll be someone else. Let's keep our eyes open in case a child needs you, needs me. I think it would make you feel better."

"I need you," Eva said. "But I am not a child. I've only done two things right in my entire life. You. And no children."

# 10

Stew Mulcahey and Dan Wisotscky were alone together.

Stew was scared. Which side was Wisotscky on? Stew felt somewhat lulled by the guy's soft tones, but then he noticed a slight flickering in the eyes. The calculation of assessment. He seemed nice, but it could easily be a trick.

"Now we will begin the individual evaluation component of the intake. Stew?" Dan asked kindly. He'd obviously settled on taking the *kindly* approach. "When you are sitting at home on your computer, have you ever gone to the Hairy Chest Page?"

Stew's face was flat, but inside he was panicking. His new plan was that if he couldn't think of the right thing to say, he would just be quiet.

"I know you met those men on the Internet. You think they're your friends, but they're not."

Stew flinched. He dug his nails into his palms. He was a good soldier.

"This might be tough for you, Stew. But some police officers from Buffalo, New York, using online names that tend to attract kiddie porn traders, collected thousands of graphic images from men like your friends. These include forty-one baby rape photographs. Would you like to see these photographs, Stew?"

Stew looked around the office. The desk wasn't as impressive as it had been when he first walked in. It was fake wood. He knew the difference. These chairs were made of shit.

"No, thank you."

"I think you should take a look. I want you to realize how sick these men are who violated you. How low they'll stoop. Once you realize that, you can put this event behind you forever. Once you see an eight-year-old baby boy being raped, you'll throw up. You'll never forget it. Would you like to see a young girl and an adult male having sex?"

Wisotscky got beady-eyed now. A fanatic. Stew definitely had to be fearful, to watch his step.

"No, thank you."

If Wisotscky was disappointed, he hid it.

"What do you want to be when you grow up, Stew?"

The thing about Wisotscky that was bugging Stew the most was the way he kept saying his name. Stew. Stew. Stooooooooo. Ooooooooooo.

"I want to work in computers."

"You like computers?"

"Yeah."

"How are you doing in school?"

"Uhhh."

"You got to stay in school to get a good job. Get your own place."

That was the giveaway that Wisotscky was on *their* side. Everyone wanted Stew out of the house; they were all in it together. But he knew he had nowhere to go. He knew he would starve and have to peddle his ass and get AIDS. If they kicked him out, he was dead.

"I don't want my own place."

No one was going to talk Stew into that. He'd get his own place, eventually. But he needed his parents. His father and mother could stop acting that way. If Wisotscky would tell them to.

"Calm down. Take it easy on your parents and then they'll calm down, too. I'm sure your father cares about you. I've seen a lot of fathers, and yours really loves you."

"Are you sure?"

"Stew." Stooooooooooooo. "Fathers aren't perfect and they make mistakes, but you have to be able to forgive him."

Stew rethought the situation. Maybe Wisotscky could be won over. This was Stew's only chance. He would just explain it to Wisotscky really clearly, and then the guy would help him. He would tell Stew's father to lay off.

"I do forgive him. And each time I forgive him, I hope he'll never do it again. But he always does. He doesn't care that I forgave him, because he thinks he didn't do anything wrong in the first place. In fact, he's mad that I forgave him. Then he does it again, anyway, so forgiving him doesn't change anything."

Stew felt good. He'd said it right.

"Look, Stew, you've had a bad experience. Everyone is upset. I can see that you're a good kid. You don't need to be in a juvenile home. Just go back with your parents and try to control your behavior. I know that seems hard, but it's easier than you think. If you ever feel out of control, stop by to see me and we'll take care of it."

Wisotscky got up and opened the door. He sent Stew a calculated fatherly smile and then called out into the waiting room.

Stew was relaxing. Maybe this guy would actually help him.

"Mr. and Mrs. Mulcahey. You can come in now."

Stew felt hope.

Brigid popped her head through the office door. Stew could tell she wanted Wisotscky to think she was afraid to come in. Her whole life was one big pretend.

"My husband is at the 7-Eleven making phone calls. My daughter had to pick up her son."

"Well, please have a seat in my office and we'll wait for him together."

Brigid came in and sat. They all looked at one another.

"Excuse me." Wisotscky got up to go to the bathroom, while the mother and son waited for Marty to get back from talking on the phone. It was like home.

*This is her chance,* Stew thought. *She can tell me right now that she knows this is wrong. Go ahead, Mom. Please, Mom, go ahead.*

His mother was thinking. But about what? Was she thinking about apologizing? She looked at Stew.

"I've got to get Daddy to stop at the mall on the way home or we won't have enough chicken, but he won't want to."

Stew started cleaning his nails.

"I remember the time the four of us went to the beach when you were little. We had a great family back then."

Stew leaned away from her, balancing his chair against the fake wood-paneled walls. The pain he felt was inexpressible. What is fake wood made of anyway?

"Daddy is too harsh on you, but he's not going to change. You are the child, you should be more flexible. I never spoke to my parents like that."

He looked up at the broken panels on the ceiling. There probably was asbestos up there.

"Why is this happening to me?" Brigid asked Stew. "No one helps me. Everything is always about someone else's problems." She looked like she was about to cry. "I have problems, too." She sniffed back her tears. He knew then that she was in control. "The day you were born was the happiest day of my life."

Stew felt a knife through his heart. She could feel that way again, right now, if she only wanted to.

Marty returned from the 7-Eleven. He stood in the doorway, panting for effect until Wisotscky came back from the john. He wanted the doctor to see how hard he'd tried to get back there on time.

"I gotta go," he told Wisotscky. "I got two customers waiting to meet me at the shop. I have to earn a living. Who do you think is paying for all this? I'm paying."

"Mr. Mulcahey, sit down for just a minute. My services are free of charge. This is a required part of the intake. I know that you care and you want things to be better. Five minutes is worth it if things get better."

"I want things to be better." Marty finally took a seat. "I got fifteen minutes. I got more."

"Good. Do you love your son?"

"Of course," Marty said. "He's my kid. Every father loves his son."

Stew felt dead. He knew it wasn't true.

"Your son is agitated," Wisotscky whispered, like he was letting Marty in on the secret of the Vatican archive. "He needs a little calm and understanding."

"Okay," Marty nodded, unsure. "I understand."

"Why don't you do something fatherly with him, like have lunch together every Wednesday? Something regular and consistent?"

"Sure," Marty said, relieved. "I can do that." He smiled. He'd gotten off easy and he knew it.

"All right," Wisotscky said, victorious. "Here's my card. Call me anytime."

Brigid and Marty stood up to leave. Wisotscky stood, too. He was tired and wanted to go home and smoke a joint. All the adults were standing, finishing, but Stew couldn't move. He was so disappointed. That should have been the greatest moment of his life—when someone would help him. But what did happen? Nothing.

Fists balled up, staring at the floor. How could this be? He had no reason to get up. He couldn't believe how he'd just been so brilliantly fucked over. He pressed his fists against his temples to keep from crying, but the movement was more dramatic than crying. He couldn't protect himself from being upset, and he knew that made him worse in their eyes. He knew it. It was a trap and they'd caught him. He started crying.

The Mulcaheys looked at each other. They were embarrassed in front of that doctor.

Stew was shaking his head.

*"You, you, you, you, you, you."*

The adults swayed awkwardly, waiting for him to be done.

# 11

Outside there was a familiar beauty of early evening as Eva and Hockey, familiarly, went off to their most comfortable spot. They shared a sentimentality for greasy diners. In part because they were still Americans at heart, but also because red pleather booths reminded these pals of their disco youths right after law school, getting breakfast at five a.m. with the ones they adored. And no matter how silly or expensive the West Village became, the diners never seemed to suffer.

It was that time of night when the most hardworking were still getting off the subway in their suits and brief-cases, while the leisure class were already having cocktails after relaxing days at the gym and advanced yoga.

*What should I eat?* was a thought Eva and Hockey shared as they slid into their awaiting slots, surrounded by streaky mirrors and depressed lonely waiters, yearning for their mothers in Albania.

Hockey's food was determined by whatever medica-tion he was on that week, and Eva's by her desire to never see Dr. Pollack again.

"I'd like something with a lot of lard," Hockey told the waiter. "What have you got?" He'd been home alone, infusing for hours, fantasizing about this moment and saying this line.

"Onion rings?" the waiter suggested brightly.

"Yeah!" One more decision out of the way. Hockey took out his pillbox. It was as unobtrusive as a piano case. "And a side of bacon. Better deep-fry that."

"And you, Miss?"

"Uhhhh, I'll have a turkey on rye with no mayo, and lettuce, and an herbal tea. Yuck, that sounds awful."

"Why not have a cappuccino?" the waiter offered, having done so well with the onion rings. He wanted to be meaningful in someone's life. "It tastes better."

"Uhh, do you have no-fat milk?"

"We have two percent."

"I'll take the tea." Then she could see how hurt he was. "I have cystic breasts, you understand."

"Yeah, yeah." The waiter was sad again and slunk off to the kitchen. Eva suddenly remembered those big, white radishes waiting at home on that lovely plate.

"So." Hockey tapped himself on the chest. "They want to take out my Hickman catheter."

"What would you get instead?"

"Well." He scratched his chest now. "I'm going to sit in the doctor's office for six hours once a week and get one big fat infusion there instead of every night at home alone for four hours."

"How great," Eva smiled. "What's it for?"

"So that I don't go blind. Yeah, it'll be great. Then after a while I won't need those long infusions at all. I'll take pills . . . or implants or something. Whatever's on the pipeline."

"Will the hole close up?"

"Yeah, there will be a scar."

"I'm sorry." The waiter was back now. He seemed devastated. "We're all out of turkey. We have ham or tuna fish salad."

"No way," Eva lurched. "Oh shit. How about a green salad? Do you have any? Of course you do."

She felt panicked about Hockey's endless suffering. She searched up and down the menu, past the drawings of the Acropolis, looking for something that had no fat. For years and years she had calmly taken in his most horrific daily life. Now, if *she* was the one to get sick, she knew for a fact that he would not reciprocate. Could not, would not—which it was remained unclear. That's how it went with these kinds of relationships—the forever ill sour to the experience of the new arrivals. They're still here, after all, so it must be no big deal. She resolved to eat anything, no matter how tasteless and vile, in order to never ever have breast cysts again and never ever see Dr. Abraham Pollack and attempt to never be the sick one in the room.

"I know," she said. "How about a salad with no cheese, no meat, no mayonnaise anything? What kind of dressing do you have?"

"Why don't you have a tofu salad?" Hockey suggested.

"I can't. Tofu has fat. Can you believe it?" Anyway, she knew they didn't have tofu in Greek diners. They had feta.

"Are you sure?" He was seriously wondering.

"I saw it on a package at the health food store."

The waiter felt suicidal. He was saving up to buy a house back home. But rent here was so expensive, the subway fare alone stole his dreams away.

"We have vinaigrette, French, ranch, blue cheese, and creamy garlic."

"Nothing without oil?"

The waiter shrugged and looked up, begging for pity.

"Okay, I'll just have lettuce and tomato with vinegar. Thank you." Eva handed back the menu, exhausted. "Hockey, I want to ask you something. When you go to the doctor . . ."

"Eva Krasner!"

An overwhelmed, middle-aged woman dragged two antsy kids over to their table. It was Sylvia, a former lawyer turned wife and mother. Eva hadn't seen her in so long. She looked good with brown hair, but tired.

"These are my children. I can't believe you've never met them. This is my son, Jehosophat. He's seven. And this is my daughter, Diogenes. She's five."

"Who are they named after?" Hockey asked obediently.

"My husband's parents, Jean and David. How are you, Eva? Still at the legal clinic, fighting the good fight?"

"Well . . ." Which explanation should she offer? The long one focusing on her own inadequacy, or just the short, sweet facts of the matter? "Actually, we got defunded."

A shroud draped over Sylvia's face. She still pretended that her retreat from the workforce was temporary, and that all the needy people and on-the-brink institutions she'd been part of would be fine without her until she returned. The news of their demise sealed her fate as a true bourgeoise who now gave nothing back, and probably never would again. She wasn't ready to believe that about herself. She was shocked.

"Really?" Her facial muscles showed her concern and panic, while her eyes shifted around to watch the kids. "I thought you'd never give up."

There it was again, the thing that had been worrying Eva for months. Had she really *given up?* Or had she simply exhausted every legal, social, political strategy possible until she was defeated by the new era of selfishness?

"I tried my best," she said.

"What a shame."

Eva was ashamed, for that was the real truth. She *had* tried her best, and her best had failed. There was, in the universe, an extant best that would not have failed, but it wasn't hers. This was the problem. She had to be better. Somehow she had to undo all the fear and limitation and become a person who, next time, saves the clinic. Or the day.

"What are *you* doing, Sylvia?"

*"Mommy, let's go!"*

Sylvia hung on to the moving children like Hercules wrestling the bull.

"Everything's great, with the kids and all. *One minute, Jehosophat!* We did kids things today. I'm taking them home from tae kwon do. Hey, congratulations!"

"For what?"

"Your sister's baby. Close call, huh? It was touch and go there for a while."

"It was?"

"All those thousands and thousands of dollars on fertility drugs," Sylvia clucked. "Enough to save the clinic, probably." She laughed. "I thought they'd have to go to China. All that expense."

"Oh."

"So I'll see you at the baby shower."

"Sure."

*"Mommy, let's go."*

"Okay, Diggie, Mommy has to pay. See you tomorrow then."

Eva watched them out the door and onto the street.

"I didn't know your sister had a baby," Hockey said.

Here it was. The one thing Eva could never outrun. Her exclusion from her family.

The strange thing was that gay people who had families told her to just give up. Not even try. Then they would go home for Christmas. They couldn't see what they had and how much it meant to them, even if it was very little. They lacked empathy.

Then there were the other gay people who also didn't have families. They told her she should be relieved to be rid of them, just settle down with her friends and Mary and forget. They usually said this over a third martini, after five excuses, three lies, four missed deadlines, and every other sign that they themselves were totally unreliable, alcoholic, and suffering daily from their own family's abandonment. And there were the straight people who say "We love you!" and you never see them again, especially not around Thanksgiving.

If the exclusion would stop, she could get over the previous twenty-four years of it. But it's hard to get over being hit on the head with a hammer every day. First the hammering has to cease, and then you can start thinking about bandages. Eva's family remained committed to earlier, stupid cruelties that they just didn't have the decency to undo. So as each event retreated into the past and there was a chance to let her back in, they would come up with some fresh, new reason to keep her out, a new wound. It was like trying to reconcile with a battering ram. They just couldn't admit they were wrong, so they had to make sure someone was.

"Mary and I only found out last week."

"That is so mean," Hockey said. "I didn't know your sister was so homophobic. Hey, I didn't even know you had a sister."

"It's complicated," Eva said. Was it worth trying to explain this to Hockey? "She gets more out of manipulating my mother's prejudices than any of her own."

"Sounds sophisticated," he said. And she could tell he had other things on his mind.

Eva had tried every strategy. She even went to the gay synagogue to find out what Judaic forgiveness was all about, but that, too, turned out to be extremely complicated. In Christian forgiveness, apparently, the offended is not involved. The victim just forgives the perpetrator, who keeps doing it, and Jesus makes it all okay. It seemed awfully convenient from the perpetrator's point of view. Jewish morality is quite different. It requires interdependence, mutual awareness, and group consciousness. Forget it. First the violator has to come and ask for forgiveness. They have to say why what they did was wrong and then they have to never do it again. The odds of getting that out of sister Ethel or mother Nathalie were basically zero. There was nothing in it for them.

"Here's your chamomile," the waiter sulked. "Sir, what can I get you to drink?"

"I'll have a vanilla malted," Hockey sighed.

"That bitch," Eva said.

"The waiter?"

"No, my sister."

"In this day and age? Isn't she embarrassed in front of her friends?"

"She tells them it's for other reasons."

"Like what?"

"Hockey, look at me."

He saw someone who could look a lot better if she tried.

"What would be a good reason to keep someone away from a child, and could any of those reasons apply to me?"

"No," he said. "There cannot be any reasonable justification for this." Then he started to imagine the kind of ritual satanic abuse that would have to be in place to keep a child away from her aunt. He was allowed to know all of his aunts, even the ones who cheated his mother on a used car.

"I love my niece/nephew," Eva said. She cried. Her salad arrived. What was so strange was that Eva truly did love this child, this unseen, unheld little being. She wasn't into children in general, but this one, deeply, was hers. She had photos to show him/her and stories to tell, and imaginary tickets to the *Nutcracker Suite*. Later the kid would hang out with her and Mary, stay over, meet all of their friends. She/he would come to Mary's plays and play Scrabble with Hockey and find out about other ways to live. Maybe he/she would become an actor, or a radical lawyer, and fight for justice and art and new ways of seeing.

And then as Eva focused this picture in her mind, she knew, suddenly, that this gorgeous image was exactly what Ethel wanted to avoid. She didn't want little darling listening to people without rights planning a better future. Ethel wanted a world where people like Ethel were the neutral center, the only way to be. This was how high the stakes were for Ethel—her own sense of herself as neutral, normal, and value free—this huge blob of Ethel's self was what was on the table. And that was something she would do anything to preserve.

Hockey stared at her plate. "Maybe I should get two malteds."

She knew she wasn't going to tell Hockey what she was feeling. It wasn't worth going into. Eva had spent so much of her life trying to understand what went wrong with her family that she had it down to a science. It was her version of the Kennedy conspiracy. She finally had come to understand how it all happened, but no one else had the patience to let her explain. She had tried to tell a therapist once. It took fifteen sessions before she got the entire story out, only to realize that the therapist hadn't been keeping track. One night she had tried saying it all out loud to Mary in their apartment as a practice for telling the world, but after three hours of solid talking, Mary was so offended by the monologuing, she made Eva promise to never do that to her again.

So she was left with no alternative but to repeat it to herself privately every once in a while, so that she—the only person who knew—wouldn't forget. Someday someone else might want to find out. Maybe her niece/nephew.

First they humiliated her for being gay, so she became alienated. Sequence, consequence.

But because the family viewed the initial humiliation as fine, Eva being upset about it was only further proof of how bad and wrong she was. Being upset about something fine was wrong. Saying that something fine was not fine was wrong. That was the familial "modus o" from 1975 to 1992. At that point, because of AIDS there was a social shift, and the kind of vulgar homophobia the Krasner family dutifully practiced went out of fashion. A new, slicker kind that they could never master came into vogue instead. So now the family brilliantly changed gears. Now they no longer cited the homosexuality as the justification for their cruelty. They now pointed to the consequences of their cruelty as its own justification. Eva being alienated was now reason enough to keep her that way. What had caused it became unmentionable.

Now she was no longer bad because she was gay; she was bad because she was hurt, because she was sad as a consequence of being hurt. Hence, no baby shower.

"So," Hockey said. "So what I wanted to talk to you about was this case I mentioned on the phone . . . Eva?"

She had to wake up.

"Yes?"

"Eva? How's your dinner?"

"Okay." She looked around. No one eats fat anymore, but they are still fat. You are what you don't eat.

"So this case has come my way. I want you to work with me. I need you."

She heard the word *need* and perked up.

"It's a good case, Eva. Internet sting, lots of juicy stuff. The kid is fifteen, the guy is forty-five."

"It's a gay kid, right?" she said, her heart open. This was why she became a lawyer. "I mean, a *gay young adult.*" A good lawyer.

"Yeah, but the kid is not our client. Our client is David Ziemska. The grown-up. All expenses will be paid by the Committee to Lower the Age of Consent Defense Fund."

Age of consent, consensual sex. She'd done that before.

"Is our client a weirdo? Does he look like a pervert?"

"We'll go out and see him next week. They're paying us fifty an hour. I know, that's nothing. It's like an honorarium. But it's more than I make with no clients and than you make correcting papers."

"I don't care about money."

"Duh." Hockey actually laughed. He had this low, gravelly voice and dark, thick hair. "It's a good case. David broke the law, but he doesn't need to get twenty-five years. He can pay a fine."

"Second offender? No way." Eva knew she was in. She caught her own face in the mirror over the counter, the one reflecting the fruit salad and half grapefruits stuffed in ice. Like Hockey, Eva was also dark, with that thick, Jewish hair she'd ironed in fourth grade and then let grow wild. They could have been from the same tribe. Now, for both of them, silver threads had begun to be their own cliché. She'd better cut it and act her age.

Would that ever happen? "Can we get the child to testify that it was true love?"

"No," Hockey said, relieved that the malted had finally come. "The kid is out of the picture. He was coerced into writing a statement claiming that he was molested, and turning in his boyfriend. I've got a photo. Stewart Mulcahey."

"Let me see."

Eva looked at herself. "There is nothing worse than being a gay kid in the wrong family." She felt closer to Hockey now. She felt a little less alone. "Hockey, I want to ask you something. When you go to the doctor and he sticks you with a needle, what does he say?"

"He says, 'This might hurt a little.'"

"Anything else?"

"'This might sting.'"

"You sure?"

"Yeah."

Eva wished she could talk more about her sister.

"Does he ever say 'Here comes a little prick?'" Was that it? "No, wait. Does he ever say 'Here comes my little prick?' Does he ever say *my* or *a* little prick?"

"I wish he would."

It was strange, the importance of that one little word. *A* little prick versus *my* little prick. She realized that the doctor had said *a*, not *my*. But as she was telling Hockey about it, she felt afraid that he wouldn't believe something wrong had happened. He would not have taken her side. That's what made Pollack such a genius. He knew exactly how to walk the line. That's why she couldn't file a complaint. The authorities would never believe her. Pollack had insured this dilemma by expertly saying *a* prick, when he really meant *my*. He insinuated his prick everywhere into her examination without even showing it.

She looked at Stew's picture again. "I feel sorry for that kid."

"Your niece/nephew? Or Stew?"

Here came the onion rings.

"You know," Hockey said chomping. "Some people do worse things to their family members than they do to anyone. They kill them, they rape them, they throw them out on their asses. You were sixteen when your family threw you out. Stew is fifteen."

"Poor kid."

"But you turned out okay. And so will he."

"Okay."

"And we'll be helping him, by helping his boyfriend, because . . . Eva? Listen to me, Eva!"

"Yes?" She was staring at the forbidden onion rings.

"*Stew is not our client*. David is."

"Check."

Hockey waved at the waiter, pointed to his empty malted glass, and signaled for another as if asking for a bottle of Veuve Clicquot. He didn't smile, and neither did the waiter. "You know what I'm worried about?"

"About Stew?"

"No, that I'll lose this protective coat of weakness I've had with my friends. That I'll be normal again, and to be normal is to be judged. Before, I wasn't accountable, because I had no future, which means no consequences and everyone dealing with you knows it. Now I wonder how long it will take before the resentment comes back."

"You're probably right," Eva said, still hungry. Actually, she knew for a fact that he was right. She could feel her own resentment already rising. Why didn't he ask her about the significance of *my little prick?* She missed her niece/nephew so much.

"Pricks," Eva said, drinking her tea. "I hate them."

# 12

When Mary Elizabeth Morgan was six years old, she inscribed her future into a first-grade composition book: *When I grow up, I will write plays.*

This vision had been revealed to her as Mrs. McKenzie's class performed *Hansel and Gretel.* It made her high. From then on she organized the Morgan family and neighbors into Christmas plays, and wrote the class show every year at Del Sol Intermediate School. After graduating as a theater major from San Diego State College, she moved to New York City with her first girlfriend (also named Mary) and discovered the invisible, under-skilled, under-the-radar world of unknown theater. She put on shows in apartments, rat-infested parking lots, and lesbian bars. Her plan was to work her way up. But she couldn't locate the next step.

Then the day came when Mary finally realized that no one in New York City enters from below.

So she tried a new approach. She now spent half her paychecks on postage and started laboriously sending out her scripts to literary managers, directors, anyone remotely connected to a real theater. She'd bring home playbills and scour the phone book, find every name that was listed and send them a script. But there was still no result.

She had come to accept the sad truth that there were people in New York City who really mattered, but she didn't know who they were. This realization dawns on many people at different points through their journey, and this was the moment it had dawned on her. These special people knew one another's certain ways, and she didn't know those ways.

She had to act specifically. But what was it?

She had to meet these people. But it had to be under very particular circumstances. What were they? Seeing them on the street and saying "hi" wouldn't do it.

She had to get in. But how?

These questions became central to her existence, and by sheer brainpower, total immersion, and focus, she began to find some answers.

At this point in the process she turned thirty. How to learn unwritten rules?

She had to be twice as good to get half as much, four times as good to get just as much, and five times as good to get ahead. Once she'd hit on these odds, Mary started workaholicking like a racing demon. She never gave up and she never stopped going. Ambition was her pep pill.

After three more years at this pace, Mary was desperate. By age thirty-three she felt—as very few people ever do—that she had taken every possible avenue to better her condition.

So finally, at this point Mary realized she was completely dependent on the recognition of strangers in order to achieve her goal. She was dependent on their grace.

She didn't need her own grace, because no one was dependent on her.

If anyone really important ever noticed her, she had to be ready to maximize it. So when she would find out about something that mattered, she would incorporate that thing into her vocabulary.

Example:

STEVE
I like your play, but it needs work.

MARY
Would you be willing to apply with me to the
Sundance Theater Lab?

### STEVE

Yes.

### MARY

(Happily)
Great! I'll call you in September when the application is due. And Steve?

### STEVE

Yes?

### MARY

If you decide that you don't want to do it, or that you want to apply with someone else, will you call and let me know?

### STEVE

Yes.

Then when September rolled around, Mary called him, faxed him, e-mailed him, and he never, never, ever, ever, ever responded. She left messages like: "If you don't want to do what you said you would do, just *tell me.*"

But he would never say no.

Finally, she dressed up as a messenger, delivered a package to his office, and confronted him in person.

"I asked, and you said *yes,*" Mary cried. "So I believed you."

"What I really meant," Steve said, looking at his

watch, "was that if someone else were to do all the work of shepherding this not uninteresting play through the system, well then, at that time the door may not be closed, especially if you get famous for something else. I was just being polite, but you clung to my kindness. You fixated on it and became so needy that I had to protect myself from your monstrous, diseased insanity."

"Couldn't you just have said, 'I changed my mind. I'm sorry I hurt you'?"

Innocent outsiders who have neither the calling to be playwrights nor the experience of being absolutely the opposite of the profile for privilege would often ask if she couldn't hold on to some small kindness. This was a loaded question. Yes, she was ultimately happy that he finally took the responsibility to say no. In fact, this was a great relief, and it helped a lot. But it did not get her play produced. And for those for whom expression through vapid but beautiful actors is the only time they feel alive, there is nothing that makes not getting your play performed okay.

At the root of this was that Mary had been raised to keep her word, so she believed what other people told her. Second-guessing them was a skill she had never acquired. She just believed what others said. If they said yes, then her investment of faith in other human beings was to believe they were telling the truth. She could not live and do otherwise.

Yet, as was inevitable, after many experiences like the one above, Mary came to know these creepy people like the backs of her hands. She could see their pubic hair through their clothes. That's how intimately she had come to know this kind of person. The Unaccountables. Mary stared at herself in the mirror. How could she become like them? She wanted to. It was the only way to have the opportunity to be herself.

Trying to learn this system was difficult. It was a new language of a subculture she had not been trained in. It was taught in some schools and some families and some circles, but not hers. So after serious observational study and consultation with various participant observers also on the hovering fringe, Mary wrote out these phrases on flash cards with their interpretive meanings on the back. So, whenever she was stuck on a subway train, or on her way home from a temp job, she would take out the cards and try to get their information through her thick skull.

Here were some of her flash cards:

— "Let's get together for coffee" actually means "Go away, I hate you."
— "Send me your materials and I'll call you next month" actually means "Go away."
— "I'll call you on Wednesday" means "Go away."
— "I'd love to see the next draft" means "Go away."

She practiced speaking the new lingua franca when she was alone, to see if comprehension would improve with practice. But when she meant to say "I'll call you on Wednesday," she just said "Go away," which defeated the purpose of the code in the first place. Because saying "Go away" made her accountable. It was easier to say "I'll call you tomorrow."

What was the bright spot in her light? Hope. No one goes to these lengths unless positive fantasy is at the wheel. Every time she tried to be like them, she imagined it would work. That felt great. Then she imagined what it would be like to be treated with respect, to live decently, and, most important, to see her plays alive before her. And that felt so sweet, so dear, so tender and right that the imagining was itself satisfying, comforting, and fun. She couldn't wait to see how good the real thing was going to feel. And it would. Feel.

If after all the joyous hope it in fact did not work out, she was devastated and had to think it all through again. In some ways she did not want to become the kind of person she now resented. But then again she did. It was the only way to not get hurt by them, again.

She had a girlfriend to cry to and cheer her on. When she tried again, Eva would say "I believe in you." Mary appreciated this, but she also knew that the words were offered somewhat in innocence. Eva, after all, was a lifelong New Yorker, and a lawyer, and although she was accomplished, she was not ambitious. Eva didn't realize what it was like to need help to realize your natural calling, how humiliating that was. Eva had been handed everything. She was born in New York, after all, and knew how to act.

Telling Mary "You can do it" and other cheers was in some ways a contrivance for Eva to feel more sympathetic, i.e., the person she wanted to be. Ever since the legal clinic had been defunded, Eva had been depressed. Mary knew she felt disappointed in herself. Eva was embarrassed by her own failure, and by the suffering it had caused her clients. Mary felt bad for Eva, but she was also sick of it. It was time for Eva to move on to something better. After all, what was happening to Mary was worse. Eva at least had a law degree; she should be able to solve her problems. Thank God that Hockey had gotten her a new gig. It was good for everyone and would keep the focus where it needed to be.

Eva had loved the clinic, and Mary had been filled with hope. Now Mary felt deep inside that there was a secret connection between Eva not being happy and no one opening the door for Mary. In a vague and unarticulated way, she felt that Eva's disappointments were exactly the thing keeping that door from opening. Now Eva had to be very, very happy so that Mary could finally make it.

After eight years with Eva, Mary had learned a lot about Jews. No matter what they got, it wasn't enough. They always wanted more. Regular white people were too satisfied. Like Mary's family. They thought that wanting anything was asking for trouble. That's why her own family didn't get her. She wished for something great, and they found that uncomfortable. Maybe that was the very attitude that kept her from knowing how to get the thing she needed. It was the hidden injury of class.

Mary's father had been afraid to want, and it didn't serve him, either. She loved him so much and wanted him to be on her side. For the last ten years of his life, she called him with every detail of hope or expectation, but he never got excited. He couldn't. He loved her, but her ambition was just a blur. He worried that she was setting herself up for defeat. It smelled to him like covetousness and being too big for your britches. It made him uneasy and it was painful to pay attention. But if he was the example of what happens when you give up on your dreams, it was a fate she wanted to avoid. Mary couldn't call him after two in the afternoon, because he would be drunk. Her mother would also be drunk. Her mother just disappeared into vague rambles about nothing.

It was so childish. Not having dreams. They were like kids. But she didn't want them to be. They were her parents, and she loved them no matter what. Couldn't they put down the bottle and reciprocate? If she called too late in the day, her dad was really out of it. But before two he was usually okay. Sometimes even gruffly funny, like when she was a kid. If Mary went to visit them in Del Sol, they would drive drunk. The few times Eva came along, she had a shit fit. She couldn't stand all the drinking and the accompanying silence. She would complain about it, call it "morose." But she would also use her credit card to rent a car so that they didn't have to ride with the drinkers. Mary's credit card was maxed out. Eva tried to help, but after two days of straight vodka and silence, she would go in the next room and watch TV until the holiday was over. She met them halfway. But Mary wanted it all.

Eva was nice when Mary's dad got sick. She did talk about "end-of-life issues," but was kind. She put Mary first. Her dad drank until every organ in his body turned to water. Mary saw him in the hospital bed, bloated, like an ocean wrapped in skin. One day the skin burst open and all the water came out. Then he died. That night, her mother went out for drinks. After that, her mother, Delilah, would occasionally repeat her dead husband's phrases, but in a more understated slurry tone. They were:

1. Get over it.
2. What are you going to do, start crying again?
3. I'm fine, I've moved on.
4. Because I don't want to.

Eva insisted all the way home that "because I don't want to" is not a reason. A reason is something like "because I'm afraid that if I try, I will fail and be ashamed." Statements that Mary and her family would never make in a million years. If she did, Eva would just respond, "You can do it." So what would be the point?

The truth was that Mary mistrusted Eva's logic system. And she trusted her parents' logic system. Even though one belonged to winners and the other to losers. But she was raised in it like she was raised to do the dishes. It was mother's milk. The trilogy: (1) ambition is dangerous; (2) praise encourages it; and (3) don't try to better yourself beyond what your folks have achieved. That's what was so heroic about Mary ultimately, so optimistic. That despite all her conditioning, she tried as hard as a person could to make herself happy. To have the life she had to have. To do what was right. She acted on her own behalf. And she hoped.

When Eva's father died, after very expensive heart surgery, Nathalie went back to school and got a PhD in education. She studied end-of-life issues among the Jewish elderly. She indulged. When Mary's father died, Delilah got a new boyfriend and a blender. She got over it. She and Tom like to make vodka drinks with orange concentrate and crushed ice or some fruit from the garden. They let Eva in the house and even sent her a Christmas card. Eva buys Delilah and Tom the most ambivalent Christmas presents possible, like soap. It's so embarrassing. How are they supposed to understand why she doesn't have the right kinds of gifts? Everyone celebrates Christmas. Nathalie and that Ethel treat Eva and Mary like dirt. But they think they're superior. That's what Jews are like. They always think they're better, no matter how they behave. That was a big part of the problems Mary was having professionally. All of these rich WASPS from Ivy League schools and Jews who grew up in New York. They run the world.

"I'm never going to make it."

"I believe in you," Eva said. "You can do it."

# 13

Driving upstate with Hockey, Eva remembered all her dreams of country houses with big stoves, a writing studio for Mary, a dog. Isn't that what grown-ups had? Someday. It would be so lovely. A picture window right over their bed so that the sun would crawl in beneath the trees, and the crisp air, coffee, pancakes, making love, going for walks, talking. The bright, quiet way. What did these houses cost anyhow? It shouldn't be too impossible. Someday.

Then Hockey turned into Ossining and she remembered her last client to reside there, Fred. The cool black senior citizen who never stopped charming and never stopped cocaine. In and out of jail well into his seventies, but somehow not pathetic. She'd get mail from emergency rooms where he checked in for diabetes, refills of Coumadin, grandpa stuff. And then he'd wrap a way-out mad scarf around his neck, find an old Nehru jacket, and look like one bright dude romancing younger ladies and smoking cocaine.

This time, though, she and Hockey were neutral, in ugly old lawyer clothes. Dull and ill fitting. They didn't talk much, listened to the radio. Clients are mirrors of lawyers' wishful wannabe selves. And David was as bland as they get. No acne or drooling; he didn't look like a monsignor or mortician. Just a regular video store clerk in his forties, a loser with someone to love. Being incarcerated did nothing for him. He didn't bulk up like most, or act tough. He just stared at the ceiling. That was depressing. This life wasn't for him; he wasn't accepting enough to figure out how to get by.

"Can you get me out?"

"I know," Eva said. "It's awful."

"I'm getting so fat, I'm growing breasts. How do I get out?"

That happened sometimes. Exercise takes motivation. Especially with all the white bread. David could pull off a few push-ups in his cell, but he was never a gym queen before and didn't even know what to do with the weights. Better to just hide on the bunk and keep very, very quiet.

Eva inhaled. This was her plan to cheer him up. That's what she always seemed to be after, helping the person in front of her out of a nightmare of unfairness. With a plan. Things never turn around without one. The forces are too strong.

"How are you holding up?"

David was panicked. "One of the weirdest things about being in jail is that you can't have conversations with anybody. No one knows how to discuss. They just take a position and repeat it over and over again. And if you don't give up, they'll stab you. No one knows how to take in information or how to negotiate."

Hockey smiled. "That's why they're in jail."

"Then why am I here?"

"What do you think?" That was Eva, being a therapist.

"People are fucked up about sex."

The two lawyers had their two different reactions to that one. *Yes.* And *But.*

"But," Hockey said, "a lot of people don't agree with fucking little boys. Take some responsibility. You shouldn't be in jail, but come on, David. Stew needs a boyfriend his own age to ruin his life."

"Just get me out of here."

"I really think we can." That was Eva. She's the one who agreed that he was being victimized.

"Great. How?" There was hope, suddenly, in David's face.

Eva felt the breeze of grace. This was her calling. People were treated unjustly. If they didn't have enough power to protect themselves, others had to intervene and help. It was the primary responsibility of being a human. It was the reason to have society. Now if only someone would intervene for Eva with her family. It had to happen someday. Maybe her niece/nephew would be the one to put a stop to this. She had to wait. There also needed to be someone who would intervene for Mary. She deserved a fair opportunity. Eva prayed there would be a person with decency and mercy who could open that door for her beloved. Someone had to intervene for Hockey. He needed better meds and didn't know how to invent them himself. And Stew. He had to get an apartment in Brooklyn somewhere and start all over again. Find a nice boyfriend to come home to who would be responsible and generous. Now Eva was intervening for David, being her best. Fighting for someone who needs it—that's what life is all about.

"I think if we work with the truth and we're smart, we can win. Our argument is fair. It's clear and true. If we explain it well, we should win."

"What is the *truth?*" Hockey snapped. She knew he'd been feeling poorly about everything and not able to get caught up in the fight yet. Maybe that's why he was being sarcastic. He was scared. That made sense.

Eva was scared, too. "That there is a double standard in the culture for May-December romances. And David should not have to go to jail for twenty-five years—or at all—just because he's an older man romancing a younger one and not a professor having an affair with his female graduate student."

"That sounds okay." David cheered up considerably. He wasn't alone, and it showed on his face.

People need each other. David needed them, and now Hockey needed her. Walking back to the car, Eva could see that Hockey was not feeling well at all. He was pissy. Sad.

"Okay?"

"Yeah."

The best thing was to not condescend. To treat him as if it wasn't happening until he said that it was.

"Hockey, is that really why you think people are in jail? Because they don't know how to negotiate? It's because they don't have rights."

"You're funny. People aren't as weak as you think."

"What do you mean?"

"Eva, you think everything is logical." He slid behind the wheel and they were off on the return through river, tree, lean steeples, whispering pines, crackle. "You just figure out what's going on, and then you explain it clearly and everything will be okay. Nothing works that way. You can't win like that. People don't just capitulate because you're telling the truth."

"It would be very good for me to learn how to fight and win."

"Winning is good. I just remembered."

"It would be a new feeling for me." All those welfare cases Eva had fought for so many years. Even if the client won, they often ultimately lost. They won a meager benefit in a no-win system.

"It's all coming back to me." Hockey was doing seventy. Breaking the rules but not expecting a consequence. "When it comes to the law, there's something stronger than truth, smarts, or love of justice."

"What's that?"

"Strategy."

They sat in the car in silence for a while, toyed with the radio. Eva didn't say anything, but she was thinking. She was remembering that strategy could win a very hollow victory. She wanted to remind Hockey of something he believed in. Something that would remind him that people's lives matter.

"If Jose had lived, would he ever have betrayed you?"

"Never."

That was the source of life, having been loved. Eva sat back, relaxed. Hockey still knew what was true.

# 14

Stew was in the kitchen boiling eggs for egg salad. Far behind there was a wind chime and incessant yapping of alien forces. He let those eggs cook for twelve minutes just to be sure. They would be as hard as potatoes and tougher to criticize. His mother and sister liked everything just so.

His mother and Carole were sitting in the adjacent living room drinking coffee. They had matching mother-daughter haircuts and dye jobs, but Carole was fatter. Although a mother herself, she had a girlish plump. Stew knew that if they stepped into the kitchen and caught him making their lunch with runny eggs, they would let him have it all right.

The two women were discussing purchases, banal details, the tiniest maneuvers. Earlier that day they had walked on a street together and shared some common topics, traded minor decisions. These were experiences that Stew would never have with his mother or his sister. He would like to, but he couldn't give them what they demanded in return. A mirror. Instead he made them uncomfortable. He was living proof of another world. Anything Stew said was viewed with suspicion. No one would identify with it. There was no way on this planet that he was going near that living room to let them look down on him. He would not give them the chance they craved to tell their in-jokes and display their intimacies. Stew would not let them raise their eyebrows and throw glances across the room at each other, even though obviously that is what they wanted most of all. They wanted to show off that they were in and he was out.

"Mom, you remember when Christina divorced Bobby, that lawyer she used?"

That was Carole.

"The black guy? You don't need a divorce. You and Sam can work it out. Just deal with your problems. Don't blame him and everything will be all right." Brigid sucked on a Carlton. "If men blame themselves, we have to pay.

They can't live with it. I don't care if everything's my fault as long as my life doesn't fall apart. Blame it on me, big deal. What do I care?"

Stew knew they were sending him messages about how *they* were the real family. Mom and Dad and Carole and her husband, Sam, and their little son, Victor. There was no question about it. They were the ones that nobody tried to get rid of, to kick out the door into juvenile hall, all the time pretending they didn't want to, just had to. Once they got him out, they would never let him back in. Then he'd have to peddle his ass and be poor forever. His mother's and sister's tones of intimacy felt heightened as never before. He began to suspect that they purposefully designed to prove what an outsider he was. They were planning it. Showing off how they talk to each other four times a day on the telephone, and that whenever his name came up, it was always as the negative example. About how terrible he is.

"Everything okay in there?"

That was Carole again.

"Yeah," Stew called back. "Lunch is almost ready."

Stew ran the hot eggs under the cold water. They were still too hot to handle. He held one in a paper towel, but it was too hot. He dropped it. Fucking egg. He hated that egg. He picked it up and smashed it in the sink, pressed his palm down on it and squashed it. It was too rubbery. He stabbed it to death with a knife, puncturing the rubbery shell. Immediately he was terrified. What if Carole came in? They'd call the police. Quickly he started scooping up the egg and wrapping it in a napkin, stuffing it into his jacket pocket so he could throw it away later at the 7-Eleven. But the eggshell pieces were too small, and he had to pick them all off of the metal sink.

He plucked the next hot egg and dropped it. This time on purpose. He stomped it. The egg squashed out onto the linoleum, and Stew admired it for one fleeting moment before picking it up with a paper towel. He propped a chair against the kitchen door, then he sponged the floor and then used the same sponge on a dish, even though that was forbidden. If anyone had seen him smash an egg, they would raise their eyebrows and then gab about it on the phone, repeating the same stupid words for hours. For years. They would never let it go.

Stew cracked another egg and peeled it. Then another. He mashed them up in a bowl with a fork and added some mayonnaise. He got mayonnaise on his fingers and wiped it on the wall. Then, afraid, he washed it off with a sponge. He couldn't breathe.

"Victor, help Uncle Stew."

Victor came in through the swinging doors wearing oversized baseball regalia, some of it inherited from Uncle Stew, like that cap that fell over the kid's eyebrows.

"I'm mad," Stew said.

"I'm hungry," Victor answered.

"Carole just wants to show off how your grandma knows every fucking detail of her stupid life." Stew peeled the remaining eggs. "I have friends who have great lives, filled with things those two corpses could never imagine. If I tried to tell them, they would be too stupid to get it."

"Like what?"

Victor had been a very strange baby. Very passive. Now, as a little boy, he was extremely quiet. Sometimes he asked questions, but they seemed to be by rote and not very imaginative. Stew never felt that Victor actually realized that life was going on.

"How is Daddy?" Carole asked in the other room. It was the question she knew Brigid wanted to answer.

"Always criticizing himself. He's never satisfied."

Stew and Victor were quiet, listening.

"This thing with Stew is making us both crazy."

*Not again,* Stew thought. It was too much pressure, this constant assault.

"If Stew doesn't get out of the house," Brigid flapped, "something terrible will happen. You remember what it was like the last time your father left me."

*I'm not going.*

"Daddy's not going to do that again." Carole lit her cigarette. "He was being a baby."

"I couldn't sleep for a year," Brigid's voice croaked. "I stayed up all night smoking."

"I remember."

"I couldn't get under the sheets. I couldn't stand being in bed. I had to weigh down one side with old coats. Every time I dreamed, I dreamed of loving your father. Waking up was a nightmare; it made me afraid to go to sleep. I cried every day for a year. My face changed from so much grief."

"I remember."

"Every night I stared at the hook in the bedroom wall and at my belt. The skin on my neck stretched. I stayed up smoking with that belt around my neck. I can't go through that again."

"How can you ever trust Daddy after that?"

"I can't," Brigid said. "But I can't trust anyone else, either. At least I know that I love him. Trust is a luxury for the young. I'd rather love him and not trust him than trust and love no one. Stew isn't the only person in this story. He's a kid. Everything can still happen for him. Not for me."

The thing about those bitches was that they had never done anything interesting. They'd never actually taken a risk and gotten caught and still not regretted it. Those two mules knew nothing about living, and yet they were in charge. How did this happen? That's what Stew would like to know. Well, he wasn't going anywhere and that was that. He didn't have anywhere to go, even if he wanted to. He needed to stay home.

"You see, Victor. If you ask those bitches what goes on in the men's room, they would say wee-wee and ca-ca. Some of the guys I meet there are from Puerto Rico, some are from Albany. If Mom knew, she would throw them in jail. Dad's trying to get rid of me, but I don't want to go. I need a home. I'm only fifteen. If he gets rid of me, I'll get AIDS."

Stew was sweating. He felt weird. The room was tipping. He was furious.

"I'm hungry." Victor looked around the kitchen.

Carole reached for another cigarette. Her lighter

jammed. "Shit." She called out. "Victor! Everything okay in there?"

Victor looked at Stew. "Yeah," he said.

Stew gripped the counter.

"Mom," Carole said. "I love you." She found the matches.

Brigid sat back in her chair. "Thank God you were born."

"The egg salad is almost ready," Stew called out to his mother and sister. Then he whispered, *"Listen, Victor, don't eat this egg salad. It has spit in it. It's only for stupid, boring bitches. They hate me, and they're going to hate you, because you're going to have a great life once you figure out that you're alive. If Mom throws me out, I might have to come live with you and Carole and Sam."*

"I'm hungry."

"How will I get food if they throw me out? Don't eat the egg salad, Victor. Have an apple."

"I want a Big Mac."

"This is a Big Mac," Stew said, holding up the apple. "Just pretend. That's what I have to do. I'm stuck in this fucking house, but I pretend I'm at the train station or the mall or the rest stop or the park." Stew was scared; he didn't know how far he could go. "Then sometimes I can escape for just a few hours and all my friends are waiting for me." His voice was strangely melodic, singing terror. "Those guys I was telling you about? What about you, Victor? Do you like guys?" There, he'd done it. Carole would kill him.

"I want a Big Mac."

"This is a Big Mac that lives in your mind. No matter how many people tell you that you can't have a Big Mac, you can have it." *Come on, Victor.* "You can smell the Big Mac. You can remember it. You can taste Mac." He got down on his knees, so close he could smell Victor's baby breath. "Believe me, Victor, get an imagination, or you'll never make it through this family alive."

"That's not a Big Mac." Victor was unsure of what he was supposed to do, and he started to worry about it.

"It is. It is. It is a make-believe Big Mac. In our secret make-believe world. Get it? In our secret world there are no creeps, there are only Macs. Hey, Mac."

"Hey, Mac," Victor laughed.

"That's our secret code, Mac. I say Mac and you say Mac and we're having a secret boner."

"Mac."

"Don't tell Carole I said *boner.* She'll tell Daddy and he'll throw me out, and I'll have to peddle my ass and then I'll get it. Okay, Mac? That's our code, Victor. The secret word only for guys." He was sweating. His tongue dried. His hands were white with fear. "Have you ever seen a really big dick, Victor? Don't tell Daddy I said that. It's you and me, Victor. It's make-believe Mac. That means we know what's out there. Guys."

"Mac," said Victor, taking the apple.

"And it's just our secret, right?"

"Mac."

"Right," said Stew, putting the spit sandwiches on plates. "Don't tell anybody." He looked at the boy. Stew knew he had to get the kid out of that kitchen. "Okay, take the bad people their food."

# 15

Mary and Eva at home. Dim light from last night's candles melted on the table. Remnants of a great meal. Wine glasses. It's morning now. Those last moments of making love again before the day just has to begin.

"Come on, girlie."

"Whoa."

"Yum."

"Kiss me," Eva said. And then, "You scare me."

"You like that."

And then the phone rings, and the bed gets left behind.

"Eva, it's for you. Some guy."

Eva could smell Mary's hair. She brushed her face against it. So soft, blonde, and light. A miracle, really, like the ocean. She ran her hand one more time over Mary's ass and then took the phone out of bed.

"Hello?"

"Hello, this is Dr. Pollack at the clinic. I was just reading over my films from last month and noticed a minuscule mass in your left breast. It's probably nothing, but for your own peace of mind I think you should go see your breast doctor and have her take a look. Even if it is a malignancy, it would be in such an early stage, but I would say you've got a ninety-nine-percent chance it's nothing. Do you understand?"

"I don't have a breast doctor. Can you recommend somebody?"

Mary got out of bed and walked over to her computer. They called it "nude writing." Eva's version was "nude housework."

"Sure. Why don't you call Dr. Gita Kumar? K-U-M-A-R. She's at Park Avenue and Seventy-second Street. She's a great doctor."

"Thank you. I'll call her right away."

"And Eva?"

"Yes?"

"Get some good insurance."

Eva looked at Mary, how sleek she was. She never tired of the familiarity of Mary's body. Its lanky shapeliness. Mary would be able to handle this. Fear of disease is a normal part of daily life. In this second the knowledge was still private. Between Eva and the clinic. She was about to tell Mary, but she looked at her first. Eva watched her.

The most important thing in Eva's life was to belong to somebody. She belonged to Mary. Everything would be all right. Nothing out there is ultimately that important when you have love. Someone to love. Each person on the planet has strengths and weaknesses. So did Mary. So did Eva. Eva accepted this. There is no person without problems; there is no relationship without conflict. As far as Eva was concerned, the difference between people who split up and people who stay together is that some people split up and other people stay together. There was no problem that couldn't be dealt with if they face it.

Whenever something disappointing had happened between them, Eva did everything she could to make it be okay. She would sit and try for hours and days to figure out what it was that upset her, what she thought was causing it, and what she thought would help make it better. Then she would prepare. This meant think it through so that she knew clearly what she felt. Then she would share all this information in a clear and loving way so that Mary could understand. Then she would sit back and listen to how Mary responded. How Mary felt. Then she would take in this new information—how Mary felt.

Mary's ideas of how to make it better. And see how this changed her own initial understanding. Eva would then systematically try all of their mutual ideas until something improved.

Like one time Eva started to feel that Mary didn't do the dishes. This made her angry. The first thing to find out was if that was in fact the case, or if it was just a false perception, a projection. She and Mary talked it over, looked truthfully at who did the dishes when. Eva was shocked to discover that Mary actually did do the dishes, but Eva had just not felt that she did. Feelings were not facts. The resentment was misplaced; it had to do with other things. Dishes had become emotional code for Eva's own feelings of inadequacy because she was unemployed. She felt bad about herself, so she blamed her lover for something that wasn't happening.

It was illustrative. How important conversation was to finding out the truth. If they had never discussed it, Eva would have blamed Mary forever for something she hadn't done. It would have been a convenient blame, and Eva wouldn't have known or faced the truth about herself. About how bad she felt about herself. How much she needed the job that Hockey had brought her, the opportunity to do something good. Then she would accept herself with more certainty and be a better girlfriend for Mary. Now it was all obvious. She was grateful.

There would always be a new problem. That is part of life. Now, with this phone call, the new problem had arrived.

"Honey," she cooed to her nude writer. "I have to tell you something. It's not bad news, it's just annoying."

"What's going on?"

"That was Dr. Pollack. He found a minuscule mass in my left breast, and it's probably nothing, which means we have nothing to worry about."

"You mean that creep who molested you? He is not a good doctor!"

"You can still be a molester and be a good doctor . . . scientifically? Right?"

Eva and Mary carefully discussed the minuscule mass for about a half hour. Mary took out her breast health book and they looked up a few things. Mary had the patience to read the relevant sections and explain them to Eva. Eva cried. Mary kissed her and looked into her eyes. And when there was nothing more to say, Mary made herself a cup of tea with a little cognac in it and kissed Eva's face a thousand times. Then Mary put the book on the kitchen table and went back to her computer. They talked some more, with Mary sitting at the computer and Eva making coffee. They discussed how Nathalie had had breast cancer, although she survived it. They discussed how they were poorer than Nathalie and had less social currency and lived in the era of HMOs, and that this added up to a shorter life span in general. In the course of this conversation, Eva admitted that dying seemed natural to her. After all, so many of her friends had done it. Even living *this* long sometimes felt supernatural. Mary was worried about the responsibility. She even said so.

"If you are dying of breast cancer, I can't take care of you by myself. And forget your family. Not after this baby shower thing."

"You're right," Eva said. "I would need a care group, like Hockey had. But I don't have cancer yet. It's just a minuscule mass."

"You're right." Mary relaxed. "Isn't this crazy? For me to have you sick and dying when all we know is that there is a minuscule mass. How did that happen? I think we had a TV moment. Isn't that funny, Eva? That we were just doing what we've seen so many women do on TV. There, when the doctor calls, suddenly the whole plot is about *Does she or doesn't she have it?* And we're all supposed to panic."

And Eva knew that was true. And she was so grateful, to have someone love her who could notice that.

"Yeah." Eva was entirely grateful. So, so lucky. "Let's not get manipulated into panicking."

"Let's not."

After all, in real life this moment is so normal. Most of the women they knew over forty had been through this, and most of them were fine. And most of the ones who were not fine dealt with it. Mary was right—they shouldn't let the TV version overwhelm the real-life one. They didn't want the TV to tell them what to feel.

"You'll come with me to the doctor, and we'll see what we need to do, right?"

"Right." Mary started typing. That was how she signaled normalcy. She had all of her most important conversations from the keyboard.

"Anyway," Eva kept talking. "A minuscule mass means early detection."

Mary could write and listen at the same time, because so much of writing is busy work, like recopying and doing cover letters. It was a way for her to both interact and release tension simultaneously.

The subject then turned to Ethel, Eva's evil sister, and the exclusion from knowing their niece/nephew. But all through this increasingly familiar but still new topic, Eva was surprised to find herself wondering if she would become a woman with one or no breasts. And if in many years Mary were to strangely predecease her, then would she still be able to get a new girlfriend? After thinking this over, privately, she concluded that if she wasn't going to die and her hair grew back, and she returned to work, she *absolutely* would be able to get a new girlfriend, just in case Mary got hit by a car.

Eva's observations of life had taught her that lesbians of her generation had sex with a lot of different people in their twenties, a serious lover in their thirties and forties, and then were alone in their fifties. This was because their lovers died, had their behavior taken over by alcohol or mental illness, went kooky for someone so young they could have given birth to her, or couldn't take city life one more day and moved to Vermont, leaving the other behind. The other, fearing boredom more than being alone, chose to be alone forever in Manhattan rather than petrifying *à deux* in Burlington. Then Eva realized she was imagining Mary's disappearance as a symbol of her own. This raging returning projection startled her. It was getting to be a bad habit. Blame.

There was a threatened aloneness to homosexuality. Everyone always predicted its inevitability. But Eva had not imagined leaving Mary behind so soon. Homosexual aloneness was an accusation, ironically created by the accusers. And then these same people went out of their way to enforce it. It was a cinch. Keeping her from her niece/nephew guaranteed Eva's loneliness, and then the created loneliness was pointed to as the inherent pathology. A neat trick.

At this point of depth between two people, it's hard to find heart for a new hunt. It's hard to be able to get to know someone new from scratch only to have to wait yet another eleven years before really caring about them. The first seven years are so preliminary anyway. Who can go through that again? Besides, how could either Mary or Eva ever explain themselves to a new person at this point? It was too complicated. Too much baggage. They each were the person who had seen the other unfold. If Eva died, someone else could come in at the end and hear all the stories—that was no fun. But if Eva lived, and only had one breast, they could continue to create the stories. And that was the point.

Mary was the person who knew all of this. Mary knew what's what.

"You are the love of my life," Eva said.

"I feel the same way." Mary looked up from behind the keyboard. Their eyes locked. Mary smiled—she felt satisfaction. It was obvious. After a minute, she naturally returned back to her work.

"Oh my God!"

"What is it?"

"Eva, look at this e-mail. Someone wants to talk to me about my play!"

"Oh my God." *Maybe everything would change at once.* "Which play?"

*"Freud Was My Co-Pilot."*

"I love that play. Who wants it?"

"Ilene Leopold."

And so that name entered their lives, electronically.

"Who is that?"

"You know." Mary was frantic. "Ilene Leopold. Ilene Leopold. Leopold. She's very well known. Someone told me she used to have a girlfriend, so I sent her my play. She produced that show—what's it called? And that other thing—you know, the cowboy thing. You saw it. With the surfers. Remember? Isn't that great?"

"Well, don't go cuckoo," Eva said, immediately realizing that was the wrong thing to say. "I mean, it's *great!* Honey, be careful. Remember what happened all the other times. Let's hope for the best and wait and see. Let's be sure this is a good person." Eva got up and touched her lover's bare back. She adored her.

"No, this is finally going to happen. Sixty-one rejections. Can you believe it? I survived sixty-one rejections."

"And the *almosts* are even worse."

"But that's not the point. Eva! The point is that I was

right not to give up. What if I had quit at sixty? Right? Then I never would have found Ilene. Ilene Leopold. Ilene Leopold. Finally, someone is going to help me who knows how things work."

Eva had a weird feeling of jealousy. This was her cancer moment, but hey, it was just a minuscule mass. It was good to focus on something more real and more promising.

"Ilene's e-mail says, 'I want to do your play.' That means she wants to do my play."

"Honey . . ."

"Don't be afraid of success, Eva, or you're going to stop me. You've got a great case now. You'll get back in the game. You'll do a brilliant job and so will I. And maybe this time around you'll be able to earn a living, and so will I."

"Right."

"So let's enjoy it. This moment, I want to enjoy it."

"So do I," Eva said with stuff on her mind. "Let's enjoy it."

# 16

Stew stood in the doorway, guilty, as Victor brought his relations their food.

"Mom, I'm worried about Sam. He's depressed." Carole put out her cigarette.

"Your father is always depressed. Just don't blame Sam, it's not his fault. Pass me the ashtray, will you?"

"It's not my fault, either. Thank you, Victor."

"No, but you can make it worse. Your father always

blames himself. He blames himself for what happened to Stew. That's what scares me. If he'd blame Stew, we'd all be a lot better off."

Stewie molested the smashed egg, lying like a corpse in his pocket.

"Mommy!" Carole bleated. "Are you saying that Sam's a lazy bum because of me? Victor, where are you sitting?"

Brigid put the plate before her daughter, as she had all of Carole's life. Just as her own mother had done for her, in that same house, until the day she died. Marty's house.

"Sam is just like your father. Don't try to upstage him. It kills them. Don't take him for granted; anything is better than being alone. Victor, did you make these sand-wiches?"

"No. It was Uncle Stewie."

"You know, Ma?" Carole tucked a napkin under Victor's chin. "I'm thinking about going back to work, part time. I hope it helps. Afternoons . . . I think Sam would be more interested in me if I got home after he does. Here, honey, let me cut your sandwich."

"If there's no one to come home to, he'll never come home. He'll stop off for one drink and that's it."

"Victor, what's the matter?"

"I don't want to eat it."

"Why not?"

"Uncle Stewie said not to. It's a secret."

Brigid reached over and cut her daughter's sandwich. "What's a secret?" She was looking for the Diet Coke.

"Grandma, Stewie and I have a secret world."

"What kind of world? Mommy, the soda's right there."

"I can't tell."

Stew was standing apart, watching his demise unfold. He knew what was coming, and he knew he should put an end to this right away, but he couldn't. Any choice would be the wrong choice. His life had fallen apart so quickly, and for what reason? He couldn't explain. He couldn't explain any of it. Every scenario seemed designed with him in mind, to tell him how awful he was and what was wrong with him. But he still couldn't figure out why. He would do something fine, and then something inexplicably, horribly, irredeemably wrong. But that calm between the two countries was so disconcerting. The danger was always there, apparently, but he didn't notice it. He just felt a tension, a light turn in the room—that was where the mistake occurred, when he went for things. If he followed a pleasure—or less, something that just felt right—suddenly . . . it was wrong. Then he'd look back, for one split second, to when it had been simultaneously wrong and right. When he felt right but they knew he was wrong but hadn't told him yet. To go from *fine* to *irredeemable* took a moment. But the aftermath of these mistakes, they were so long and slow. The punishment seemed to go on forever. Here it was, happening again. A slogging toward inevitable punishment for one moment of one bad natural decision.

"Stewie!" Victor was worried. He couldn't take the pressure.

"What's going on?" Carole was very still.

"I can't tell you." Victor was losing it.

"What do you mean you can't tell me?"

"Uncle Stewie said not to."

Carole looked at Stew. He knew his expression was wrong. Insolent and hopeless.

"Well," she said, coldly, "I say that you need to tell me."

"Victor?" Brigid asked, calmly. "What's the matter?"

"Stew!" Victor just started blubbering. It was awful for everyone.

"Stew!" Carole lunged. "What is going on here?"

"Nothing."

She slapped him.

"What the hell is wrong with you? What did you do to Victor? What did you do to him?"

"Nothing."

"Don't tell me *nothing*. Don't tell my child to keep secrets from me. What did you do to him? There is nothing my child can't tell me. What did you do, Stew? Did you molest him? Oh my God. What did Uncle Stewie do to you, honey? Tell mommy. Did he pull down your pants? Did he touch your penis?"

Victor was staring blankly. He put the apple to his mouth.

Stew did not have the resolve to fight her. He had the courage, but not the skill. But he needed to say something. Everyone was staring at him, like they always were, demanding explanations, but for what?

"I told him there's a secret world where there are no bitches."

"Secret? What kind of secret?" She didn't get it. "Don't bullshit me, Stewie, or I'll have you locked up."

There it was. She'd let the cat out of the bag. All along everyone had been trying to get him locked up. They were dying to do it. They all said so, openly. They were just waiting for the right chance to pounce. It didn't matter what he said or did. It was inevitable. They wanted it that way.

"It's a secret world."

Carole looked at him with confusion. She was making a decision. She could have just understood that nothing bad had happened and been okay with that. Been his friend. But then she would have lost all that special ground she'd gotten with her mom. All the conspiracy. She'd have lost all the points she'd gotten for getting pregnant, just like her mother, and then getting Sam to marry her, just like Brigid had with Dad. She could have that special status if Stew was twisted, a pervert. If he was okay, she'd lose everything.

"Mommy," she screamed. "Mom."

Stew looked up and saw his wary mother. Her worn, sagging face. He could tell that she'd wished Carole had not called her to duty, but now that she had, his mother had to play her part. That's how it went for Brigid. She took what she could get. If Carole and his father didn't pressure his mother to hurt him, she wouldn't. But once they expected it, she had to come through. That was the decision she had made, and now it was too late. She was getting older. She was fatter than before, but not so fat as

Carole. Her face was more wrinkled than ever. She had no patience anymore, because she'd learned that there was no payoff. Ever. She'd tried to be flexible when Marty had that affair, and look what happened. Now she knew there was no more room for flexibility. No allowance. Everyone had to stick to their role.

"What did you do to that child, Stew?"

Stew knew it was all over for him, because everyone else's positions were at stake.

"Please help me," he said. They could do it, Carole and Mom. This could be the moment when they could just decide to help.

"If you didn't do anything wrong, defend yourself."

What did that mean? He couldn't figure it out. How can he defend himself if he didn't do anything wrong? It meant the attack was coming from some other source. It had nothing to do with him at all. He didn't cause it, so he couldn't control it. The attack had its own willpower. He couldn't stop it.

"I can't. I don't know how. I don't know what would work."

"What are you talking about?"

He shouldn't have said *boner* to Victor. He should have just kept his big trap shut. Of course Victor liked guys, but Stew just shouldn't have said so. That was the problem with everything—that it's true. Why couldn't Stew ever learn the lesson—that what is true must be kept a secret? To say anything true is wrong. That's the point. What's right is wrong. It was all his fault.

"There's something wrong with me. I'm wrong."

Brigid looked so tired. She was too tired for this.

"I'm going to ask you one more time, Stew. If Daddy were a fly on the wall in that kitchen, would he be upset at what he saw and heard? Yes or no?"

"Help me, Mommy."

Carole grabbed her mother's arm. She owned her.

"All right, Stew." Brigid was disappearing in front of him. "You made your decision. You had all the power to make this family work. Now the rest of us have to react. It's over for you, Stew. Nobody wants you here."

# 17

Mary was right. Her life was going to turn around now, so Eva's had to, too. This was it. Things were finally going to go their way.

All night Eva thought about David Ziemska and how to get his charges dropped. She imagined the final courtroom scene, where the judge would realize that Dave shouldn't be sent to jail, how happy they would all be.

She imagined going to the pay phone in the hallway

and calling to share the news with Mary—and then not calling her mother, because Nathalie would be offended. Or calling her anyway, hopefully, and then confirming that she was in fact offended. That she considered Eva's victory to be depraved. That she looked at what was right and thought it was wrong.

How did this happen? It was in many ways an accident of history.

When Eva was sixteen, her father caught her lying on a bed with her high school girlfriend, Ilse Goldfarb. He ranted and raved all over the house, he was so mad. He said Eva was a homosexual because she had hit her head a lot when she was little, playing rough in the schoolyard. It was caused by her concussions.

He screamed at Nathalie, in front of Eva and twelve-year-old Ethel, that it was Nathalie's fault. She had turned their daughter into a homosexual by loving her too much. He said Nathalie and Eva were too close. All of his pent-up rage from years of feeling excluded was unleashed on the three females who stood watching their family fall apart, having to make choices. He said Nathalie had wrongly taken her to hear Martin Luther King, thereby causing her deviance.

None of these females were ever the same again. Nathalie stopped loving her daughter immediately. The consequences were more than she could handle. Choosing her daughter would have meant being a failure, a failed ex-wife with a damaged child. Ethel vowed to never be the object of criticism, no matter what the price.

And Eva? At first Nathalie privately hoped that by no longer loving her child the homosexuality would wear off. She hoped, subconsciously and semiconsciously, that if Eva had no mother to count on, she would turn to men and become normal. There were a couple of times over the years, but not many, where Nathalie suspected uneasily that Eva might be right about something, but she would never say so. She just could not take a public stand for Eva. It was too painfully reminiscent of that homosexuality that everyone knew was Nathalie's fault.

Later, after her husband's death, Nathalie came to believe that homosexuality was not caused by bad mothers but was instead a genetic mutation that can't be helped. This brought her some relief. But she never fully let go of her late husband's bitter words. After he died she phoned Eva from time to time, when she felt lonely. That was the best she could do. Anything else would have meant she and her husband had been wrong, and she couldn't live like that. They had to have been right, to have had the best marriage and the most incredible life. Anything else was unbearable.

On the night of this original accusation, twelve-year-old Ethel sat on the floor of the living room behind the couch, crying. She watched her sister be humiliated by their father. This was the sister who babysat for her, who took her to the park, who watched out for strangers, who took her to museums and movies, who had held her hand as they crossed the street. This was the sister whom Ethel had always asked, "What's going to happen?" when they watched television shows. This sister had stayed up late at night telling Ethel about the world and sharing philosophical discourse. Ethel had worn her hand-me-down dresses and shoes. This was the sister responsible for buckling her seat belt.

Now this sister was tainted. She was bad news. Eva was now a very frightening person, because what had happened to Eva was the worst thing Ethel could ever imagine.

The only way to have a family was to shun Eva. After a while it became a habit, the way things were. Then everyone got used to the new family of three. In fact, it turned out to be better for Ethel in the long term, no competition. Soon, letting Eva back in seemed absurd, unnatural. Eva's world become further and further away. Ethel had no curiosity about it. The equation was closed for good. That's how those things go.

To get in with the parents Ethel had to be anti-Eva on all questions, no matter what. It all turned on that moment when their father criticized Nathalie for too much love. If she stood up to that father, Ethel would not have a family, either. Eva wasn't getting one. If she stood up for Eva, Ethel would be the second child for the rest of her life. The choice was clear.

Eva's removal from the family benefited Ethel on all fronts. Strangely though, as happens with this sort of thing—the intimacy of the subject toward the object— Ethel followed in Eva's rejected footsteps, even as she colluded in keeping her out of the family for the next twenty-four years. Ethel also became a lawyer. The kind that does divorces.

• • •

The next time Eva and Mary made love the television set was on. There was a story in the background of their pleasure and both of them were secretly listening to it. It was about a doctor who had won a prize for a new invention. He diagnosed a mental health condition called *Folie à Trois*. It was based on a family that had been brought into his hospital by the police. The family members all thought they were lions. They growled and walked around naked on four paws and ate raw meat. The doctor discovered, though, that when he separated the mother, the father, and the child, only the father really thought he was a lion. The others just imitated him. When they got away from him, they had the chance to act normally again. They just wanted to be with him so much that they imitated what he did, took on his flaws. That was the situation with Nathalie and Ethel. They lived in a closed system inside a world of possibility.

Many times Eva had wondered what would have happened to her life if she had actually done something wrong so many years before. Could it have been worse than what they did to her for being gay? This particular sleepless night with Mary by her side, Eva could still not imagine a worse result, even if she had stabbed her teacher. At least then her family would have come to visit her in jail. Now she looked at what was happening to David Ziemska. What if she had had sex with an adult instead of with Ilse Goldfarb? Probably it would have been better. They could have blamed it on the adult. That's what happened to Lord

Alfred Douglas, or that kid in the Edmund White novel, or David Ziemska's little boyfriend. All those guys turned in their lovers under pressure. That's what happened to Ilse Goldfarb, to Nathalie, and to Ethel. Pressure. Ilse got married immediately at the age of eighteen in a time when no one like them did such a thing. But this was a quarter of a century in the past.

"I thought things were supposed to change."

"Who told you things changed?" Mary was sleeping. It was like typing. Mary could sleep and talk at the same time.

"I saw it on TV. It's better for homosexuals now."

Mary laughed in her sleep. "Right, on TV everything is better. Turn off the set, though, and it's the same old shit."

Eva tried to close her eyes.

"Ilene, I'm sleeping," Mary said. "We'll talk about it in the morning."

But Eva knew they wouldn't. In the morning she would call Dr. Gita Kumar and make an appointment. Then, perhaps, a whole new world would begin.

Eva lay in the darkness. Some birds started to sing outside the window. That meant the sun was coming up, and when she looked, she could see the leaves emerging quietly from the weedy trees outside on her street. Her block would soon start to come and go. There was a decent beauty about her life. Something elegant and great. Whatever happened at Dr. Kumar's she could handle it, because Eva Krasner was loved.

# 18

Turning in off the street there was a rehearsed, polished gleam in the refurbished lobby and then emotional chaos in the dingy elevators and hallways. That's what entering a hospital repeatedly is like. As the visitor nears the room, she engages the realm of faintly rotten, lukewarm bad food and the undertones of fuzzy television sets with afternoon talk shows. Visitors are numb, and patients weak. Workers are underpaid, doctors distracted.

The first thing Eva did when she arrived at Hockey's hospital room was to give him a kiss on his dried-out lips and look slowly into his eyes. They were as inflamed as bloody sunsets.

"It's the experimental drugs that they infused me with in the office," Hockey said. "The dosage was too high and they poisoned my eyes."

He had the same impassive expression he had always had when he was in the hospital all the previous times over the many years. But now that he was supposedly better, it was a bit harder to take.

"I have to dilate my pupils every two hours so that if by some chance they freeze, they will freeze open."

"Oh, I get it." Eva took off her coat. "Then what are they going to do?" She unloaded all of her legal papers and scratch pads from her huge briefcase.

"Then they'll try again with a lower dose. I can read, but slowly, with a magnifying glass."

"That's okay, I'll read to you. Can I use the phone?"

Eva dialed and was now pushing the various voice mail buttons. All the speed-up engendered by computers, faxes, and phone machines was slowed down by the impossibility of dialing one number and speaking to one person. She tried a shortcut by pressing "0," hoping to outwit her historical moment and actually get a real person. But of course the system outwitted her and she had to start all over again.

"Sure. The thing is, they claim they can stabilize my eyes with lower doses, but how can they do that if they already did this?"

*Your call is important to us. Please do not hang up. An operator will be with you shortly.*

"How can they?" Then she pointed to the phone. "I'm on hold."

Eva didn't bother Hockey with her life, but she had been on hold for weeks trying to get through to her insurance company. Dr. Kumar was nice on the phone, but very expensive. Eva couldn't even schedule the examination until she knew for sure what the insurance company would do about it.

"I mean, I'm already at the end of the pipeline," Hockey said placidly. "There's nothing left that works for me, so I have to try anything new, no matter how toxic. Why aren't you shocked? I know the answer to that question."

"But are you still better than you were?"

"Yeah. Don't you think so?"

"I think you are." Being on the phone was no obstacle to conversation these days. Most people holding phones to their ears were actually on hold.

"I am. I'm better. I guess so. Much better. Lucky to be alive, I guess." Hockey shrugged in his pajamas.

"Okay." Eva shifted receiver shoulders. "Let's just pick up where we left off last time, and if the insurance company ever answers this phone call, I'll just deal with it then." She sat back in the visitor chair, receiver scrunched on her shoulder, going through her notes. "I want to argue *selective prosecution.* That if David had been involved in an intergenerational *heterosexual* relationship, the courts would not be asking for twenty-five years. In fact, if Stew had been involved with an older woman, in most situations his family would be winking and patting him on the back."

"Better be careful there," Hockey said, groping on the nightstand for his sippy cup of water. "If the judge can locate one case where some straight person got punished, your argument goes out the window."

"I'm ahead of you. I found the Miller case. A thirteen-year-old boy had sex with his forty-year-old female teacher and impregnated her. The court sent her to prison. But, Hockey, can the judge really use that case against us? Stew is fifteen, not thirteen. No one got pregnant, and David wasn't his teacher."

Hockey was methodically trying to find the cup.

"Obviously this straight person was way out of line," Eva continued, allowing him the achievement of finding it himself. "Miraculously she got punished, probably because it was a woman. That doesn't mean blaming two guys for being in love is fair just because one way-out straight woman got punished, too."

"I know. Where's my water?"

"Three o'clock."

"Thanks."

"But it's hard for the judge to see the differences." Eva watched Hockey with concern but stayed blasé. "They're always looking for the one extreme exception to prove that homophobia doesn't exist."

"They don't understand comparisons. Like how I'm comparatively better."

"Yeah," Eva said. "You know, those judges think they're being fair if they rule half the time for landlords and half the time for tenants. But the landlords are wrong ninety percent of the time. The nuances of justice are what elude most people."

The nurse's aide, Mrs. Hernandez, came in with Hockey's lunch on a tray. He smiled and waited politely until she left the room. That was one skill all frequent hospital-goers quickly learn—to find out the names of the aides, how the TV works, how to move the food tray, where to store his wallet.

"Should we bring in experts? Get that food away from me, the smell will make me throw up."

"Okay, here—hold the phone." She handed over the receiver and moved the tray. "What about the fruit? You might want it later."

"Okay, leave it on the windowsill."

Eva wheeled the food out into the hallway. "God, Jose left you great insurance."

Una Owens, another aide, came in to change Hockey's sheets.

Throughout his illness, Hockey was constantly horrified at the way that black people and Latin people had to clean up his shit, serve his food, and administer his medication. He didn't want to be in that position, and yet when push came to shove, here he was. When Jose died, his whole family was in the hospital every day, speaking Spanish to the Dominicans on staff. It made everything easier. They knew each other's relatives and talked a lot

about old friends and new. But now that Jose was gone
. . . If Hockey was sick at home, he did everything himself, even if it took hours. But once you're in the hospital,
that's it. There are servers and served, especially for
people with decent insurance. The end.

Eva stood out in the hallway with the phone cord
pulled tight. She couldn't go anywhere, but she wanted
to leave Mrs. Owens and Hockey some privacy. She
looked out down the hall at the faraway window. There
was the East River and FDR Drive. She wanted a cigarette. She was still on hold. There must be some way to
show the judge what homophobia looked like so that he
would be able to recognize it in this case. But it was so
difficult to represent. Any judge with a TV had seen
some representation of homosexuality. But nothing
showed the homophobia. That's what she and Hockey
really needed. The only movies she could think of were
the ones where the person who hurts the gay guy turns
out to be a repressed homosexual himself. That wouldn't
work. It let straight people off the hook.

*Your call is important to us . . .*

Mrs. Owens finished her tasks and Eva stepped back
into the room. Hockey was depressed, she could tell. He
was still, depleted. He couldn't see. The sadness was so
familiar. The resignation like old times.

*Please do not hang . . .* "Hello? This is Shelley
speaking."

"Oh my God, Shelley? Don't hang up. Do you know
that I have been trying for six days to get someone on the

phone?" Eva could never move from one disaster to the next. She wanted justice for all of them.

"Can I help you?"

Shelley was already annoyed.

"It's this letter I got from you. I might need to have a surgical biopsy, and I'm trying to figure out the cost."

"Well, do you need it or not? If you don't need it, we won't reimburse."

"Well, I can't go to the doctor to find out if I need it until I find out how much of that visit would be covered. You see, it's a Catch-22."

"What's that? A diagnostic code?"

"No, an expression from the sixties. According to your letter, my doctor's fee of three thousand dollars would be reimbursable for twelve hundred dollars? The facility fee of four thousand dollars would be reimbursable for six hundred? What kind of insurance is that? . . . All right." She sighed.

Hockey was dilating his pupils. "What's the matter?"

"I'm back on hold. It's so hard for people to conceptualize beyond their task."

"I just had a revelation."

"What is it? That I need new insurance?"

"No. We won't get justice by showing the unfairness," Hockey said, holding the dropper over his eyes. "Because they can't see things that way. If we bring in five thousand examples of men being severely punished for sex with consenting minors and they have one case of a straight woman sent to the slammer, then we lose. But we would deserve to lose, because we're appealing to a sense of justice that isn't there. We're hallucinating. It's wishful thinking. We're deluded . . ."

"And therefore . . . ?"

"We have to appeal to their egos, not their hearts. Our truth is too difficult to explain."

"Oh shit."

"What's the matter?"

"Fucking Shelley disconnected me. She disconnected me." Eva sat down on the bed. "Do you have room under the covers?" She hung up the phone and lay back on his pillow.

"You know, Hockey, I feel so insecure about so many things. I cringe at the end of every day. I never know how to act. I have trouble making the right decisions. But there's one thing I really know, and that's the law. I think if you really work with the truth and you're fucking smart, you can win. And I really, really want to know what it's like to win."

She kicked off her shoes and threw her feet up on the bed.

"Maybe it'll be fun," he said, lying back to join her. "Pass me those canned pears, will you? I guess I'm feeling better."

# 19

Brigid was afraid of what she would find when she got back from work. On one hand, she hoped that Marty had taken care of everything. That he'd called Wisotscky and that Stew was already out of the house. She would have stayed home and packed Stew's stuff, but she couldn't miss another day. Mr. Soto had made that very clear. He needed her, since she was the only one who knew how the invoice system worked. Those days off she'd taken because of the Stew thing were screwing up everybody on the job, and they had let her know about it one, two, three. Threatening to bring in computers. Those computers were the devil; they ruined everybody's life.

When she walked in the TV was on. That was a good sign; it meant Marty was home. For one year she had walked in every night to nothing. Nothing. She came up the walk, turned her key in the lock, and heard nothing. There was no point in even going in the house after that. It would just be another night of desolation. That year while Marty was gone, all day at work she'd dream of coming home and hearing the TV on, then she'd be there and it would be off. She spent many hours sitting on the front step weeping, unable to enter. Or crashed in a chair at the dinette set, sleeping in her coat, clutching her keys.

But now the TV was on, Marty was home waiting for her. Her man was home for good.

"Hi, honey," Brigid said. He looked so young, like when he first came back from Cambodia. "Is everything okay?"

"I don't know where Stew is. He never came home. I took the day off to talk to him, like we said. I wasted the whole fucking day here and he never came home. What, he just ran out the door?"

"I told you. When Carole confronted him about Victor, he just ran out the door."

"Well, I don't know where he's been all night."

"Did you eat?"

"I microwaved that meatloaf."

"Good, it was for you."

Brigid went into the kitchen and helped herself to some food. Then she opened a Diet Coke and came back into the living room.

"What are you watching?"

"Some crap."

She hoped Stew would go out and earn his fortune. Meet a nice girl, get married, have kids. Someday they'd all drive up in a big car for Thanksgiving and everything would be all right. She'd cook a big ham. She and Marty couldn't help him; he had to get out of there and do it on his own, get a job. He was big enough. She had worked when she was just a kid. It's normal.

"Marty?"

"Yeah?"

"They hired a new manager today and it wasn't George."

"Why not?"

"Because of his drinking. I told you. So guess who got it?"

This was the life she loved. Coming home from work to the sound of her husband's TV. Eating dinner together, talking over their day. She'd worked all her life for this.

"Who?"

"Guess!"

"Who?"

"Why can't you guess?"

Marty pointed the clicker like a gun. "How am I supposed to know?"

"Either you're helpless or you're not. Which is it?"

She hated herself the minute she said it. She knew it was wrong. "Oh, Marty, I'm sorry. Please."

Brigid wanted to get down on her knees in front of him, beg him for forgiveness. Rub her face into his crotch, bend over on the carpet before his desire. Stew was gone now, so he could fuck her in the living room. He could make her asshole bleed. She wanted him to fuck her in the ear, so that her brain would come out the other end. She hated her own mind. She couldn't stand it. She'd cut her tongue out if he would smash her brain with his penis. She wished she could rub her face in it, that he would beat her with it until she was black and blue. She wanted his dick to be enormous, a two-by-four, filled with nails to gouge her heart out. Why couldn't he just beat the shit out of her? Fuck her and stab her a few times? Hit her over the head with a hammer? Then everything would be all right. He'd feel better and she could relax.

"You. You got the job."

"No," she said. "It was Louise from purchasing. She wants to cut lunch from one hour to forty-five minutes. I told her that's why it's called a lunch hour, not a lunch forty-five minutes."

Marty raised the volume on the TV. He was channel surfing with the volume up. It was like he was fucking her in the mouth and her head was banging against the wall. A battering of partial sound. No sense, no relief, no control. Then he stopped.

"Look at that man ride a horse."

"What is it?"

*"Red River."*

"Is that John Wayne?"

"You know damn well it is. Please give me a break, Brigid. I can't go five minutes without you telling me what the hell is wrong with me. I can't live with that, do you understand? I'm doing the best I can. I don't want to hear what's wrong with me. This is it. I'm not getting better. I don't want cops and shrinks and wives telling me what's wrong with me. I can't do anything about it."

"You've only got one wife as far as I know."

Brigid went into the kitchen and got some more supper. She came back to the living room resolved to try a softer tone.

"Kathleen at work is pregnant. Don't tell anybody."

"Where is Stew? I don't like this. Why is he running away?"

"He must be guilty."

"I know he's guilty. Our kid is sick." Marty stared at the TV. "Now he's gonna get it."

# 20

There were clean magazines and up-to-date newsletters in Dr. Kumar's waiting room. Everything was so crisp it was disconcerting. Efficiency overkill.

"You're the youngest person here," Mary said, and Eva found that comforting. They were having the same observations, even with new and upsetting experiences. They were still sharing assumptions. Eva felt reassured that if worse came to worst, Mary would let her have the mastectomy, all the chemo and other toxic medications. She wouldn't ask her to go to an Icelandic faith healer and eat quinoa. Eva had the kind of personality that was only compatible with official medicine. New Age worked for holistic people, but partial people needed radiation.

"I wonder if all these cancer waiting rooms are the same," Eva said. "Average age, fifty-five. I haven't been the youngest in years. I feel so strange."

"About having breast cancer?"

"I don't have breast cancer." She looked around the room. How many women were wearing prostheses? "No, about going through this and no one in my family having any idea."

"So tell them." Mary started reading a strategically placed list of support groups. She seemed hurt.

"Mary, honey, we talked about this five times, and we decided together that there was no point in getting them involved."

Of course Eva was whispering. It was a murmuring kind of environment, and these very lesbian conversations were habitually muffled. Nobody wants to hear two female lovers talk about anything real, and no one wants to hear them struggle with each other. It was instinctual knowledge, fear masquerading as privacy.

"They don't love you and they're not going to help you. They don't know you and they don't respect your feelings. For God's sake, they wouldn't even invite you to the baby shower. How are they going to help you when you're dying of breast cancer?"

Five other patients looked up at that point, and Eva realized that breast cancer was something that had happened to some of them a long time ago. Those were their good old days.

"I don't have breast cancer. I have a minuscule mass." This line was starting to feel ridiculous to say.

"But what if you do have it?"

"I don't know. You mean what would I do tomorrow morning? Have breakfast. Be freaked out. Go to work. Help you."

"Help me what?"

Something was going wrong all of a sudden.

"Tomorrow's your meeting with Ilene," Eva said quietly. "I want it to go well."

"It's the beginning of our new life."

"I'm so glad." Eva held her hand. "I hope this isn't the beginning of my new life. I don't want to be afraid."

"Of what?"

"The fear, the pain, the details."

"What kind of details? You mean what if I'm not good enough?"

*Oh, that was it.*

"I know you love me," Eva said truthfully. "And that's what no one else can do."

"When my father died, it was horrible. I'm just not that experienced with doctors. I don't know how to make those decisions."

*Listen. Listen,* Eva told herself. *She's telling you how she feels. Believe her.*

"You're right, we need to keep my family out of it."

"I want to tell you something," Mary said, feeling heard, putting her forehead on Eva's forehead. "I am your family. I will take care of you. Don't ever speak to them again."

Eva looked into those soft blue eyes. Yes, that was the truth. Mary is her family. Someone in this world cared about what happened to Eva. Someone was accountable. Mary.

The receptionist called out *Eva Krasner.* Eva stepped behind the divider and into the expensive presence of Dr. Gita Kumar.

She had planned this conversation for a while now, and yet was unable to carry it out in an orderly and expected fashion. So after only a few minutes of one-to-one contact with Dr. Kumar, Eva, again in an examination gown, opened her big fat mouth.

"Excuse me, there is something I want to tell you about Dr. Pollack, the doctor at the clinic."

"There does seem to be a tiny presence here on the film," Dr. Kumar mused, with her back to Eva, in the light of the fluorescent mammogram. "It looks like some microscopic mass inside of a milk duct."

Eva felt nauseous. But why? She was a grown woman, so was Dr. Kumar. This kind of thing, being molested by Dr. Pollack, shouldn't throw either of them. Everyone knows it happens regularly. So it had happened to her. Other people had spoken out about it, and now she was going to do her duty.

"You see, he gave another patient a bad result on the phone in the middle of my breast exam. I mean, right in the middle."

She had decided to start with this fact, the most outrageous and believable, before getting to the prick part. Eva had concluded that almost anyone in their right mind would agree that this part of the story was wrong. Morally wrong. Then she could tread into the murkier waters of innuendo, where it would come down to *Lesbian Accuses Religious Father/Doctor.* That would take more than luck to pull off. There would have to be no God.

Dr. Kumar turned her head but not her body, and posed like a supermodel on the cover of a Karachi fashion magazine. She smiled a dazzling smile. She was wearing nail polish. Deep red.

"I'm sure it was nothing."

"I think it was something."

Kumar stopped still and stared at her. She was slightly cockeyed. She wasn't glamorous. Actually, she looked exhausted. Sloppily, Eva told the story of the phone call, the never-ending breast exam.

"That's crass," she said, plucking the film off the light wall and coming closer to Eva's barefoot, infantilized, fearful body. "But he's a nice guy. Stop looking for justice and take care of your health. We can do a surgical biopsy, or we can just watch it. Your chart says your mother had breast cancer at forty-nine. You're forty. It could be at the microscopic mass-in-a-milk-duct stage."

"Wait and watch? That feels right. I'm not a good fighter."

"Well, better learn. You don't want your first real fight to be for your life. Think it over."

Kumar was done. She'd recited the Miranda rights.

"Do you think I should have the biopsy?"

"It's very early." She was patient. "If we do a biopsy and find cancer, it would be easily treatable. It most likely is nothing. You can save yourself the surgery and just wait and see if it grows. I can't make that decision for you."

*Grows?*

"I can't wait and watch anything," Eva said, sweating. "Surgery is my only option, emotionally."

Back in the waiting room, Mary was sleeping. Eva was so happy to see her. She could accept Mary's limitations—of course she was exhausted by all of this. What was the good side? Despite hating doctors, feeling inadequate, and having a generally difficult time giving herself and others a break, Mary had still come to this waiting room and done her best. Mary was there when Eva needed her, and that made this whole nightmare so much easier, even though it was still hard. Eva felt reassured as she reached for her checkbook. The receptionist was madly answering the phones. Everyone in New York seemed to have cancer.

"How much do I owe you?"

The phones were wildly waving.

"Three hundred and fifty dollars."

"Do you take HIP Choice Plus?"

"No HMOs."

"How much is this surgical biopsy going to cost? I know this is an expensive business."

"Dr. Kumar's fee will be three thousand dollars. Hold on . . . Dr. Kumar's office. Hold on, please . . . Dr. Kumar's office. Hold on, please . . . The facility charges four thousand dollars, plus you have to have a wire placed in the breast on the day of surgery at another facility. That will cost about fifteen hundred plus lab fees."

"How much is the lab?"

"I don't know. Hold on. Dr. Kumar's office."

"What insurance do I need?"

"We don't recommend insurance. Hold on. Hello?"

Eva looked at Mary. She was stretching.

"Wait, do you take Oxford?"

"What? We bill to Oxford. Dr. Kumar's office, please hold."

"Okay, I'll go get Oxford." She kissed Mary on the hair. "Honey, wake up. Everything is going to be fine."

"I knew it," Mary said and smiled.

"Everything is taken care of now." Eva kissed her. "I just need to get one more small thing, and then it will all be over."

# 21

Stew ran—he did not make a decision. He was not in charge of his actions anymore. As he felt his body turning, he knew this was the wrong thing to do. That it was irreversible, the flight. That, irreversibly, it would lead him to more disaster of such supreme dimension that he was compelled to run toward it. He fled out the door and into his dark, unavoidable fate. His parents' actions had sealed his future. He gave in and he ran.

Stew ran until he was out of breath. Then he walked down to the park, panting and sweating. There, some boys he did not know were playing basketball. He sat down and stared at them. Their light, dancing ease and their tense insecurities. Both attributes naïve. He was not naïve; he saw everything now. Their stupid competition and dull put-downs. They sped up before him and lost some of their dimension. Slowly their faces and personalities merged, and instead he was taken over by the swirling sneakers and their competing brand names, the white skin like beige clouds. There was no time anymore, just a sea of short swooshes moving through the air. Punctuating sweatbands.

Then it was dark, and suddenly he was alone on the bleachers. He had hypnotized himself, but the trance wore off, so he started walking back toward his house. It was a blind plunge into the darkness. It wasn't too cold out, and he could hear the crickets chirping, the buzz of electrical devices, TV sets, and a couple of cars gliding around corners, the sound of garage doors opening automatically. No sighs or moans of pleasure.

He climbed into his father's garage and breathed in the smell of oil and gasoline. He felt like puking. Then he lay down in a corner with his head against the cold concrete floor. Did he sleep? What does that mean?

In the morning Stew got up and went to school like an automaton. It was weird. He was dirty and had no books, but no one seemed to notice. He hadn't handed in any homework in a few weeks anyway, and had become one of those kids the teachers expected very little from. But he did get some lunch. It was delicious grilled cheese and French fries and milk. He washed his face in the boys' room and slept through sophomore English. After school he just went back to the park and watched basketball again.

This was the kind of life his parents wanted him to have. Repeated nothing day in and day out. This is what they had done, slept through school and watched the game. He had the ability to do that forever. It was how he was raised, but he didn't want to. Now it was evening again, and Stew was freezing this time and starving. He slowly climbed off the bleachers and headed home.

Stew was afraid to make a decision—he didn't know how. Everything was topsy-turvy, and any move would have been a bad one, but he couldn't just stand still. He tried it, standing very still on the corner of his subdivision, under a streetlight. The electronic buzz became deafening, he thought he was going insane. He couldn't go home. He had no money. He was hungry, having long before consumed the squashed, pocketed egg.

Did Stew have a friend? He wasn't sure. David was his friend. There was a girl in his chemistry class whom he admired. She was smart and loud. She deflected the attention, which made him feel safer. But she was black, and he didn't know where she lived. She was the only black girl in his class. Who was her father? Some black guy somewhere. He just wanted to go online. It was the only way he knew how to relax.

Stew finally accepted for real that he couldn't go back to the house. Trouble was waiting for him there. It all started to come together—what was going wrong. Everyone around him was mediocre. They couldn't do anything they wanted to. And they were mad at him because he could.

It was shocking, this revelation. His family was a bunch of bores. They weren't happy, and nothing interesting ever happened. That buzz of the garage door was the soundtrack to their life. Then he got it, and fear stalked his soul. Stew realized that the more his family understood how truly different he was, the more they were going to want to remove him. He had to get out. But how? Where would he go? He could go to Joe's house, but how would he get there?

It hit him then—he couldn't go to Joe's. Joe and David were in trouble because of him. Stew couldn't go near them. He was surrounded by walls, his family, the police. No one was flexible. No one had a reasonable explanation for their behavior, and no one had to. It was crazy.

In this way Stew started to take in that he was completely and totally alone. He had no mother. He had no father. He had no sister. He had no boyfriend. Everything had been taken away from him for some reason he couldn't understand. Everything that everyone else in the world had every day had been taken away. It made no sense. He looked at the lights protruding from houses on both sides of his street. Each of those people had families and lovers. He was the only person on this block who did not.

He thought ahead to his future and saw nothing. There was no achievement, no maturation, no old parents proud and happy. No Carole to barbecue with, no Joe or David to snuggle up with and suck their cocks. There was no birthday. No Christmas. No money. No food. No dinner. No phone calls. Maybe his mother and father would die soon and Carole would let him back in the house. But when would that happen? It could take a long time. Then what would he do if his parents died? He needed them. If they died, they would never change their minds.

There was only one person who could help him. Who would outlive him, who everyone seemed to listen to. That was Victor. He needed to talk to Victor. He needed to get Victor on his side.

Stew turned left instead of right and went down the block to Carole's house. Where was Victor? The car wasn't in the garage. That meant Sam was out drinking as usual and Carole had taken Victor somewhere. But where? Stew then decided to go back to his house, get some food, clean up, and pack his stuff. He turned again and walked down his block, up his walk. He had walked this block and that walk for fifteen years. His whole life. He had always thought of it as his, but it wasn't his. It belonged to his father. He had to take his stuff and get out.

When Stew got to the front step, he could see that the TV was on. It glowed through the drapes. That was the sunlight in this life, the TV. It illuminated every path. He put his hand on the knob and opened the door.

# 22

Mary waited for Ilene Leopold to return her phone call. She had been waiting for weeks. Each morning she left for work with seven dollars worth of quarters, calling her own answering machine from every third working pay phone to see if Ilene had left a message. If she got sent out on a temp job that had e-mail access, she checked her e-mail every ten—no, nine—minutes to see if Ilene had sent any.

As each day passed, Mary became more possessed by strategizing about Ilene Leopold. After all, Ilene was the key to the life Mary wanted to have. Her real life. Everything before this next moment was a waste—it was just treading water. Because after Ilene Leopold kept her word, Mary would cease to be a discarded person whose plays would never be seen, and whose calls would never be answered. She would become her true self. Mary knew that later, when her play had had a moderately successful run and she and Ilene were on their next, really big project, Mary would buy a cell phone and one of those handheld e-mail things, but that was then and this was now.

"Hockey is having problems again. He has growths all over his face that have to be frozen and burned off. He's depressed."

Mary calmly watched Eva talking, but inside she was screaming, *Ilene, Ilene.*

"He's always depressed, but who can blame him?" This was Mary speaking in code about herself.

"The fact is," Eva said over her morning coffee, "we've lost our preliminary pretrial motions because the judge is Catholic. It's a fix. If the judge were Jewish or black, we'd have a chance. We're going to have to settle. David isn't going to like it, and neither is Thor."

Eva loved talking like this over breakfast, sharing the amazing journey toward solution with the most interesting person she'd ever known. No one Eva had ever loved had had to come as far as Mary had had to come.

She admired this so much. Eva loved this strength, all that vision in one little person.

Mary had to keep her message-checking to herself. If Eva knew about it, she would go bonkers. Since Eva did not have big dreams, she had no patience for another scheme gone awry. Well, it wasn't that she had zero dreams; they were just about things like rent control. She was able to do what she was put on this earth to do, so she didn't understand how crucial it is to someone's soul when they are kept from that pursuit, as Mary had been. Mary had always known that false hope was better than no hope. "Dwell in Possibility," Emily Dickinson had said, and look at what a great writer she was. A big break can only happen if you try.

"The thing is," Eva said from her cup of joe, "if this were a heterosexual adult male and a girl child, I know I would feel differently. But when it's two gay men, I don't know—the romance serves another function."

"What's that?" Mary asked, thinking about Ilene Leopold.

"Well, a lot of gay people felt like aliens in their families. The structures did not always serve them. But gay children need parents, too, and sometimes gay adults are the only ones who can give that kind of knowing love."

"But sex . . ." Mary said.

"I know. But isn't there something sexy about having parents for kids who are straight? They watch them sleep together, live together, kiss and hug. They hear them have sex and probably watch them doing it, too, catch sight of their genitals. Straight kids get all that porn at home, and gay kids have nothing to look at. Why wouldn't gay teenagers want to have sex with gay adults? They need parents and friends and their own private peep show."

"What are you going to do about tomorrow?"

"You're coming with me to the clinic, aren't you?" Eva panicked. "You're going to meet me there at one, right?"

There were a lot of cars honking outside. Something must have happened. It reminded Mary that there was an outside.

"Of course, but I mean, aren't you nervous?"

That morning Mary had gone for a run along the river. The air was so sweet, just a light breeze peeking around the boats. Over her shoulder, the skyscrapers looked scrubbed. They were gorgeous. But even this image laid out before her wasn't enough. She knew that without opportunity she would always be a spectator. And that would never be the right life. Never.

"I'm terribly nervous," Eva said. "I'm terrified that I have cancer. I'm afraid that tomorrow I'm going to come out of that clinic with breast cancer, and then it'll just be me and you dealing with it. We'll be alone. Are you afraid of that?"

"Yes," Mary said. "I am afraid." She seemed little, vulnerable. A soft, trying love. Eva's heart was so open.

"But you are not alone," Mary said, reaching for her sweet. "You have me."

Eva listened closely. This was what she had dreamed of her entire life. She watched those lips say *You have me.*

And yet she was thinking, guiltily, adulterously, that she also wanted her niece/nephew. Was that wrong of her? Was she letting Mary down by still, after all this cruelty, wanting to have relatives? Would this subconsciously make Mary feel unloved?

When she left the house for Hockey's office, Eva stopped at a pay phone and called Nathalie's number. It was strange to dial it after so much time. It made her sick, the familiarity.

"Hello?"

That voice. Eva wanted to be a good daughter and slit her own throat.

"Hi, it's Eva."

"Hello."

"Did Ethel get our present for the baby?"

*Yes,* Eva hoped she would say. *That was very thoughtful. We know it's been hard for you, being kept away from the family for so long. But I can see that you really love the baby, and I've told Ethel that this exclusion has to stop.*

"I don't think a black T-shirt with the words *Iggy Pop* on it is appropriate for a baby, do you? Ethel says it's some kind of Satanic cult."

A particularly noisy truck came by at that moment, so Eva had to hunch over the phone, pressing one finger against the other ear, keeping out every influence but Nathalie's.

"We thought it was fun."

"What do you know, Eva?"

"You know, Mom. You're right. I know nothing."

"Well, you're right about something."

Eva kept her voice even. "What's the kid's name?"

"Maison Toibyn Levi."

"Any chance of me and Mary getting to come visit . . . Maison?" She clutched the pay phone's slimy receiver.

"Eva, Ethel doesn't want you influencing her children, and I agree."

"Influencing them to do what?"

"You know . . . going against their parents."

That was it, after all this time. Eva's conjecture was actually right. It was fear of the other world. The world of people who know that the rules don't matter, or are wrong or boring or unfair. Homosexuality was at the centerpiece of this other way of seeing, and Nathalie took it as a personal affront.

Would it be worth it to have cancer if that got her a mother? Too late. The days of deal making were over. She had no mother and she never would. She did not want cancer. Someday she and Mary would see their niece/nephew and the three of them would talk.

When she hung up, Eva called Mary.

"Guess what?" Mary said on the phone, ecstatic. Happier than Eva had ever heard her. "Ilene Leopold is on her way over."

"I'm so glad," Eva said, deciding to keep her own problems to herself. "I knew you could do it. I believe in you."

Back home Mary was preparing for Ilene's arrival. She cleaned the whole place and bought great food: fresh mozzarella, Israeli tomatoes, gorgeous bread. She changed the sheets, just in case. She went to the expensive deli and got olives and hot peppers, and when she came home fifteen minutes before the meeting, there was a message on her machine.

"Hello . . . Mary? It's Ilene. I'm feeling dizzy and won't be able to come over. But, Mary, if you call me exactly on the hour, we can have a phone conference. I'm really, really sorry, but I'm really, really sick."

Mary stood under the clock in the kitchen and smoked. The hands ticked, ticked, ticked. She called as the church bells struck, but she got the machine.

"Hello? Hello? Ilene? Ilene? It's Mary. It's three o'clock. You said I should call you at three o'clock. You said you were really, really sick. It's three o'clock—whoops, it's three-oh-one. I'll call you back."

Obviously she hadn't done it the right way. Something was not working out. Mary considered all the possibilities: Ilene could be asleep, or in the bathroom, or even in the hospital, or dead. Or maybe it was that same old thing again, where the person doesn't mean what they say. Was Ilene just another liar in Mary's life? What was the right way to talk to a liar? She couldn't figure it out. What was the way to get Ilene to keep her word? She waited ten minutes and called again. The machine was no longer picking up. Someone had unplugged it. Another nasty trick.

An hour later, Mary's phone rang. She stood there, smoking, watching the fax come in.

Dear Mary,

You're treating me like a child.
Love, Love, Love (and I really, really mean it)
Ilene Leopold

The only sane response would be to smoke crack. But Mary wasn't sane. She didn't know where to get crack, and she wasn't sure of exactly what it was. All she wanted was a no. Screwing around with someone's artwork was just awful. Many cigarettes later, Mary came to a realization. What Ilene did was terrible. And yet she got away with it completely. There was nothing Mary could do.

Snap.

And then it all became clear.

Had Eva been playing a horrible joke on her, too, making a fool of her? Day after day, year after year, Eva kept encouraging Mary to do what she wanted, to work on her plays, to schmooze, to go see plays, to have readings, to send out manuscripts, to talk to agents, to actors. Eva pushed her and pushed her. But Eva should know that Mary was never going to make it. That people like Mary didn't stand a chance. She was in the wrong class. That's why she had cautioned her about Ilene. Eva *knew* no one would ever really let her in. She *knew* it. It was obvious. So why was she spending years pushing Mary to do something that was going to fail? To commit to a world where she could never succeed or excel. It was a sick joke. Eva was treating her like a trained seal. She just wanted to see her bark.

When Eva came home that evening, she said the words "I'm scared about tomorrow." But Mary was seething. She didn't feel any empathy.

"Get over it," she said. Then the phone rang. She grabbed it. "Hello? Ilene? . . Oh, Mother?"

Instinctively, both Mary and Eva looked at their watches. Delilah never called this late; she would be too sloshed.

Something terrible must have happened.

"What?" Mary looked up at Eva. "What is it, Mother? Tell me." Mary loved her mother; she always had. And at this second she knew it, entirely. Mary knew she wasn't alone if she could love someone that much.

She listened and breathed softly. She felt her own compassion and responsibility and whispered to Eva, "*Tom died* . . . I'll be right there, Mother. I'll pack right now and go straight to the airport."

Mary was wanted. She was good for something.

Eva touched her hair.

She sat in the chair and watched Mary pack her bags.

"I guess you're not going to the clinic," she said. "Hockey will go with me." Strangely, Eva felt relieved.

The phone rang once. Stopped. They both looked at it.

"Maybe that was Ilene," Eva whispered.

"It wasn't Ilene."

Mary packed enough for four nights. "I was thinking about when I was twenty. The San Diego State College Theater Department. I had no idea; I thought it would be easier."

No one in her family knew how things worked. There were people on TV; her family sat and stared at them. Maybe she could be on there, too, and then they would look at her with something other than disapproval.

"You had a romantic view of your own life. That's beautiful. You deserve that." Eva saw an airplane pass between the stars. She wished on it. "And our life has turned out to be worth it."

Mary added a notebook. Then took it out and left it on the desk. She added a book to read instead. "I thought I came to New York to make it and fall in love. But now I think I was just pushed out of Del Sol, really."

"That's not the truth." Eva rocked—it was her favorite chair. "Honey, you had choices and you had awareness and you were active; you made your life happen. Don't take that away. Every morning you choose our life. You reach for it, and engage it, and deepen it."

"How do you know it didn't just happen to me?"

An ambulance passed, sirens wailing. Someone else was having a catastrophe.

"I was thinking about you this morning." Eva rocked. "I was thinking about how when we first got together, you told me that story about all the girls you had sex with when you were in high school. How you used to get them to kiss you in the movies. I loved it; it was a great story. I didn't realize until years later that it had never happened that way. You wished it had. So then you came here and made it real. I admire that girl so much."

"That solitary, horny oddball?"

"I admire you."

Mary took one pair of pajamas. It was hot in Del Sol. "I keep reaching for that normal life, and it never happens."

"What's a normal life?" Eva's voice was lulling, but her eyes were glassy.

"Something I don't have," Mary said. "And I don't know how to get. Something you can sum up."

"That's what we have," Eva said. Her voice was as soft as the wind on a hot, lovely beach day, the wind on the skin of the woman you love. "We give each other meaning, even if it's only in private. When it's just the two of us, we have so much. You say the most beautiful things to me."

"Like what?"

"You say 'I'm so glad you're here.' And 'I am your family, I will take care of you.' You say 'our niece/nephew' and 'dinner's ready.'"

The suitcase was packed. Mary felt a strange, abstracted sentimentality that could easily become forgiveness, responsibility, and compassion—or it could just as easily get filed away.

"Okay."

"Call me as soon as you get in."

"Okay."

"Mary?"

"Okay."

# 23

"Please stop, Daddy. Please."

"Stew, what you did is serious, it's criminal."

The room was churning around Stew, and for the first time he saw the color of the furniture, brown and green. The drapes were beige. This wasn't his home anymore. It was just a place. His father's miscomprehension was so unbearable that there was nothing else Stew could stand to notice. He wanted to go deaf and blind. No sight of his disappointed, angry, hurt, sad father.

"Daddy, please just stop saying that. Just stop, for five minutes. Five minutes, five minutes."

"Don't tell me what to do," Marty said for the fiftieth time. He kept repeating it over and over. No matter what Stew said, Marty took it as an insult. "I'm ashamed to even think of what you did to Victor. What should I do? Should I call the police? I was so happy when you were born. Just ask anybody."

"Daddy, please stop saying that."

"Shut up." Marty couldn't negotiate. He didn't understand how it worked. "You can't have it both ways, Stew. Either you've got nothing to be upset about, or you got to pay the piper."

Stew was very still, trying to figure out how to explain to Marty to stop saying mean things so that they could talk about what really happened.

"I can't decide until you stop." Maybe that would work. There was too much pounding on him; Stew couldn't get a grip. *Stop it. Stop. Stop.*

Marty put his hands on his hips, then he swung them around, like he was trying to fly. "Life doesn't work that way. You got to get control of yourself. It doesn't depend on me."

"Stop saying that. It's making me insane. I'm going to kill you."

"You're going to kill me? I'm going to kill *you.*"

"Daddy."

"I know you, and I know you are the kind of person who would hurt a little child."

Stew started to cry. "How do you know?"

He showed his pain, how successful his father was at hurting him. He showed his father that he had won, that the purpose of these insults, which was to defeat Stew, had worked. So now he could stop, the winner.

"Because, Stewie, you have secrets."

"So do you."

"That's how I know."

Stew saw a blur of yellow out of the corner of his eye. It was his mother, her hair newly dyed. She had been sitting there all along but hadn't said anything, like a lamp. But now she was standing up.

"You're crazy," Brigid said. "You've got to get out of this house. Now. Get out. Good luck."

Marty picked Stew up. The kid wanted to be touched, but not to be thrown away.

"I've had it with you," Marty said, lifting his son like he was a bag of laundry.

"No, Daddy!"

Marty started dragging Stew toward the front door. Stew struggled and then kicked. He wriggled free. Stew was screaming. Marty grabbed him by the arm and dragged him back. Then Marty opened the front door. Stew grabbed onto the door frame. He dug his heels into the carpeting and tried to be heavier. The carpet held him back, but then his legs buckled and Marty pulled him, sliding on his knees against the carpet, up to the threshold of the house. Stew grabbed a table leg, but it had no anchor and the table turned over. On it was a lamp, some magazines, and a can of Coke. The Coke spilled and the lamp fell over. The magazines slapped onto the floor.

"You bastard," Marty said.

Now they were at the threshold again. Stew grabbed onto it, trying to keep his father from throwing him out. He hooked his foot inside the frame and clawed at it. His father pried open his son's fingers, the way he'd counted them when Stew was first born. Then Marty reached down and grabbed Stew's foot and pushed it out of the house. He pushed Stew down on the front step and slammed the door.

It was suddenly quiet. Marty didn't know what was going to happen.

"This isn't what any of us wanted," Brigid said.

Marty was panting. He felt awful. He felt so sad, he couldn't bear it. Marty bucked up. He was too old for this. What could he do now? "He calls me Daddy," he said, hands outstretched, helpless to Brigid. "But what is he, a man or a boy?"

"Don't blame yourself," she said, not going to him, letting him sweat it off. "We've had a happy life. You tried everything. This is his problem. He'll straighten himself out. Don't worry."

Stew sat on the front step, backward, looking up at the closed door. He was disappearing. Something was happening to his skin. It was changing; it changed color and then it started to tremble, slide, and disappear, reappear, then finally be gone. His body was running, but he was not running. His mind was closed. There were no thoughts. He looked at his pants. They were torn. How would he get new ones?

He stood up and walked down the block.

As Stew walked he saw all the shapes of his life. Those flat, white rectangles where his enemies lived. The long green tubes of lawn, the squares of cement. He saw the round, blank faces of his enemies. Heard their threats. He saw their throats. They waved at him with bloody hands. Breathing was hard.

# 24

"I can't believe I've got this wire sticking out of my tit."
Eva felt strangely relaxed.

It was Hockey's first day trip out into the world after
coming home from the hospital. A surgical biopsy for Eva
felt like just the right thing. Something light.

"I can't believe we had to go to another clinic to get
it and then take a cab, with you in your robe, to this clinic
for the actual biopsy. Who thought of this?"

Eva held his hand. "Welcome to the wacky world of women's health care."

"It is its own monster."

As they sat in the second waiting room, Eva imagined Mary getting off the plane in California. She knew they would talk on the phone that night, each sharing their own story about mortality. If this biopsy was positive and she had to have a mastectomy, or worse, would she tell her family, and would her mother come to see her? That family that had never helped her, would they visit? Would Ethel finally bring little Maison Toibyn so that a dying Eva could pat him/her on the head? Would cancer bring them back together again?

Hockey seemed better. He was a great person to have through all of this. Clinics were mother's milk to him. He had no anxiety and knew exactly how to act. It was easy. She'd seen Jose's pain and Hockey's pain, so pain wasn't foreign, the horrifying naturalness of it.

If there was going to be a second half to her life, what was she looking forward to? Mary. Anything else? The truth was that Eva was not excited about being a lawyer, fruitlessly helping people who would never be treated fairly. There, she'd admitted it. Perhaps being sick was a way out of those prisons we choose to live in, like the wrong career.

"Do you ever feel that dying would be easier?"

"I *know* it would," Hockey laughed. He felt so comfortable. "But death may not be my fate."

They were sitting in the very feminine waiting

room of the pink clinic on the tony pastel Upper East Side. All the upholstery, carpeting, and wallpaper were floral. The chairs were dainty, really too small for most behinds. The décor was intended to make the patients feel feminine, even as they were about to get carved up. Even though almost all would never, ever feel that they met or could meet the feminine standard that the décor proclaimed. It was the famous double bind, the one that showed up in every part of life. This promise, waved in front of her at the moment she was least able to fulfill it. Like the existence of the niece/nephew she had never seen and yet loved. Or her mother, who wouldn't live forever, but felt no pressure from that fact to start being kind. These promises were tangible, and yet impossible to obtain.

"Any advice?"

"Well," he said, thumbing through *House Beautiful*. "If you do get sick, just keep working. I stopped and it was a big mistake."

"Or take a trip with Mary around the world."

"Yeah, then go back to work."

They looked so normal, the two of them. Like the other men waiting with their wives. People approved. The other men were thinking about their prostates, their cholesterol, their mistresses, their angioplasties, their future and past strokes. Hockey fit in perfectly. He, too, was on a new medication.

"How do you deal with uncertainty?"

"I can't," he said. "From time to time I prepare for

different outcomes that seem certain, and then they don't come true. It's dislocating, the lack of explanation. Sometimes, though, the craziness, the wild ride is actually exhilarating. Once you get used to constant terror. I have a limit. I mean, we all do. But most people never have to reach it. I know how much terror I can endure."

"So what do you do when you pass your limit?"

All the paintings on the floral walls were of flowers.

"I have to become another person," he said, like someone else would say *Pass the salt.* "Someone who can endure it. And the old Hockey is never seen again. It's happened a couple of times. You want to know the three most dishonest words in the English language? *Get over it.* If you're a conscious person, you can't get over anything real. It changes you."

"Yeah, I noticed," Eva said.

The waiting room was filled with solemn old ladies and their half-dead husbands. This was the end of the road and they knew it. If this was to be her tragedy, it would be a clear one. Something that everyone would understand and acknowledge. Something to which they would respond appropriately. Not like the nebulous tragedy of her family that no one could define. Mary was the only family Eva had ever known. Mary. She was so real. She was the only real thing in Eva's life. She was right there in Eva's mind. The feel and width of her.

When Eva went in for prep, she saw Hockey smile and wave. The orderly sedated Eva, and she was wheeled into surgery. Right before she fell asleep, she saw Dr. Kumar's face looming over her, smiling. Dr. Kumar was nice. She made a joke and Eva laughed. Then she fell asleep.

That night she called Mary, but no one answered. *She must be at church*, Eva thought. *Or maybe at the bar.*

# 25

Stew tumbled up Carole's front walk without hesitation, even though he wanted to hesitate. He wanted to stop and think things over carefully, weigh all the options, but he couldn't. There didn't seem to be any options. In a way, he just forgot. It was all already in motion. What was logical or right didn't matter anymore. This was a different kind of world now.

Stew knocked quietly on Carole's door. Then he walked around in a circle. Then he rang the bell. He did that for about fifteen minutes. One knock, one circle, one ring. Finally he went around to the backyard. Carole was sitting there in her lawn chair drinking a Diet Coke and smoking. She was watching a small TV, propped up in the kitchen window, plugged in over the sink. She was acting like she was inside, but she was outside. The only concession being her ugly pink-tinted sunglasses. She looked so familiar, Stew loved her.

She had been there when it happened; that made them close. The incident that never took place. The non-event. Somewhere inside of her Carole knew what the truth was. She knew he hadn't done anything to Victor; she just had to pretend to get Mommy's approval. But now it was only the two of them, so no more lying. She would have to fess up and stop all that pain.

Then, for no reason, Carole made the decision to start screaming. Accusations are always easier than telling the truth.

"What are you doing here? What's wrong with you? Look at you. You're a mess. Don't come around here looking like an insane person." She didn't move from her chair.

Stew pretended to leave, but he did not leave. He turned like he was out of there but actually walked into the house through the garage. He knew she would think he'd gone home. But she didn't realize there was no home. That now this had to be his home, because she lived there. She was his sister. He had to be with someone who knew him, so this was it.

Stew locked the doors to the yard, the garage, and the

street. He didn't want her yapping to interrupt this very important talk he had to have with Victor. Then he went into the living room, where Victor was on the couch playing with his computer.

"Hi, Victor."

Why wouldn't Victor say hi? He knew better than anyone that Stew hadn't done anything wrong.

"Come on," Stew said, and he picked Victor up roughly by the arm, but not as badly as his father had just done to him. So why was Victor complaining? Why did he complain if Stew wasn't hurting him the way Daddy had? Daddy had done much worse, and yet Stew hadn't complained about that; he didn't complain about the pain, just the insults.

Yet, here was Victor, not having anyone yelling insults at him, so why was he screaming? Why was the kid screaming? Didn't he know that nothing was happening?

Stew knew Victor was doing this just to get Carole to come into the house. Victor was a squealer and a tattle-tale. He was just like the rest of them.

"Shut up, Victor. Shut the fuck up."

Stew slapped him.

"Shut up, you fucker."

Stew put his hand over Victor's mouth and squeezed it.

"Shut up, or I won't have a home."

Victor yelled, and now Carole was screaming from the other side of the house. It was too late, though. Why did Victor have to do that to him? The little shit. Stewie hit Victor in the head.

"Shut up, Victor," Stew said, pulling his arms and

swinging him around. He could feel the little boy's arm slip out of the socket.

"Shut up, you little tattletale."

Then Stew felt worried.

"Please shut up," he said. "If you would just shut up, everything would be all right."

Carole was banging on the door of the house, but Stew had locked it.

Why can't people just stop doing stupid things? Just stop it? If everyone would shut up and listen, Stew would have a chance. They all needed to listen and stop saying cruel things, things Stew couldn't take.

"Shut up, Victor."

Stew tightened his hold on Victor's mouth. Victor was gurgling.

Here comes Carole, screaming again; all she ever does is scream. Now she was banging the plate glass with a baseball bat and climbing into the living room through the broken window.

Stew held Victor between himself and Carole. Victor was like a chair or a garbage can. He would protect Stew one way or the other. Victor flew around the room, Stew holding on to his arms. Victor's head hit the wall. Carole ran to him and Stew grabbed the bat. She wouldn't let go of it. She reached for Victor and still held the bat. Stew pulled on it. Then he got it and it swung around. He grabbed it and swung at Carole. She fell down. Then he hit Victor on the head. He smashed Victor's head and dropped the bat. Then he ran out through the shattered picture window.

# 26

Stew ran to the other side of the park, but when he got there he forgot why he had come. So he lay down under a bush. He noticed that he was bloody, but he wasn't bleeding. Dirt was clinging to the blood. He was crying, but in a way he felt better. He had shown how he felt. After all this time of keeping everything bottled up, he had gotten angry, and he felt a slight relief. But now he was afraid. What if something really bad had happened?

They would never get over it. Victor would be okay—he was just scared. But what if Stew had to go to jail? He would get AIDS.

Stew imagined the trial. He saw himself in handcuffs, feeling so scared. If there was a trial, the judge would find out in court that it was really Stew's father's fault and Carole's fault, because they never listened. The judge would cross-examine them. And they'd have to answer, because it was the law.

"Mr. Mulcahey, what did you do when Stew begged you to stop insulting him?"

"Objection, Your Honor."

"Objection overruled. Answer the question."

"I didn't do what he asked."

"And what, Mr. Mulcahey, would have happened if you had done what Stew asked, if you had stopped insulting him?"

"My son would have gotten a fair shake."

"Thank you. No more questions, Your Honor."

Stew suddenly looked up. He had been daydreaming or sleeping or something, but a lot of time had passed. There was an afternoon chill and it was threatening. His legs and hands were sore and swollen. His shoulder hurt terribly.

Stew knew he had to find someone he could explain things to so that all of this could get cleared up. Then his father would be nice to him and Stew could go home. He couldn't call Carole; she would be mad about Victor, and she would never admit that the whole thing would have turned out differently if she hadn't put him down. He couldn't call David, because David was in jail. He couldn't call Kevin Bart—what a moron. Maybe he could hitch a ride to the mall and trick with some guy in the men's room, and maybe that guy would help him. The problem was how dirty he had gotten and how much everything hurt. No one would give him a ride, and then he'd have to deal with mall security, who probably already had their eyes on him. They'd turn him in in a flash. Then he decided to go see Dr. Wisotscky.

"Sit here, Stew," Wisotscky said, shutting down his computer. "You look terrible. What happened to you?"

"I got in a fight."

Stew started to cry.

"I see," he said, picking up the box of tissues and placing it at Stew's disposal. "I'm glad you came to me about it. That was the right thing to do. Now, why were you fighting?"

"He wouldn't stop insulting me."

"Well, did you walk away?"

"No."

"Why not?"

"I couldn't walk away; he wanted me to walk away. If I had walked away, he would have won by getting rid of me. I wanted to stay."

"But, Stew, you can't control other people. It may be frustrating for you if another boy at school doesn't want to be your friend, but you can't make him do it. You know, these are hard things to learn, but we all have to learn. Let me tell you something. You're into computers, right?"

"Yes."

Stew looked at Wisotscky's computer. He wanted to steal it. How come the old man got a computer and Stew couldn't have one?

"Look at my computer. At first, when I was gathering data for my studies, I set up a camcorder on a tripod and pointed it at the screen." Wisotscky laughed good-naturedly at himself. "I didn't realize I could save it to a disk. At the beginning I was really stupid."

Stew was speechless. He was getting worried. This guy wasn't helping him.

"That's how it is with you, Stew. You are at the beginning of your life. In a way, you're stupid. You need to learn that people can't be forced to be your friend. No matter how frustrating they may be."

Stew was exhausted. He was ready to cry.

"What are you feeling, Stew?"

"I think I'm in trouble."

Wisotscky made a note. He wrote the word *guilt*.

"That's not a feeling, that's a thought." Wisotscky had his fatherly cap on. "A feeling starts with *I feel*. If you start with *I think*, that's a thought."

Stew shut up.

"You're young, you're bright, you have your whole future ahead of you. Now you're having some problems at home and at school. But you have a choice, Stew. You can either see your problems or emphasize your gifts. You can see the glass as half empty, Stew, or half full. Half empty or half full. Half empty or half full."

The phone rang. "What'll it be? Huh, Stew?" Wisotscky swiveled in his chair and picked up the phone. "Wisotscky . . . Yes. Lieutenant Bart?" He listened. "Oh." He looked up nervously at Stew. "Yes, yes I see." He ran his hands over his scalp and then took out his handkerchief and wiped them. "I understand completely." He hung up and looked at Stew.

"Was that my father?"

"You know very well that it wasn't."

"Okay, so there's something wrong with me." Stew was crying. "My father hates me."

"Your father is an asshole." Wisotscky was nervous. What did this mean about him? He folded his hands and clenched them. He could lose his license over this. "You're responsible, Stew." He looked up at the boy—he was lost. Stew had no idea of who he had become.

"What do I do now?"

The social worker stared. He felt pity. It was so intimate, this moment. Soon the police would come, but right now it was quiet. "Stew. I'm sorry. Nothing can help you but mercy."

# 27

Hockey unlocked his office door at eight thirty the next morning to find Eva fast asleep on his desk. The lamp was on, and she held the telephone in her hand. The desk, chairs, and floor were cluttered with half-written letters, notes for half-written letters. Some of these failed, regretful missives had even been sealed in envelopes before being crumpled and tossed to the ground. Some even with stamps. They were accompanied by discarded pens and many cartons of bad take-out food of such poor quality the consumer clearly had to be out of her mind with grief.

"What did you do? Spend the night here? Did you get a bad result from the clinic?"

It was Hockey's second day back in the office on his new new medication and his new new required dietary regimen. He'd brought a kelp salad from home, a decaf no-fat latte, a protein bar, and an apple. It felt great to swing his briefcase, to tie his tie, to grab a cab. These actions boondoggled the guillotine.

"I don't have cancer," Eva smiled.

"That's amazing!"

He kissed her and squeezed her.

"Mary won't answer the phone," Eva said quietly. Then her face fell apart.

Hockey shut off the lamp and turned on the light.

"I'm so glad you're okay," he said, emphasizing the good, while knowing that the heart is a different kind of ache than the lymph node.

"Thank you."

"Is she still at her mother's?"

"I don't know."

Eva's eyes had receded an inch into her head. She looked like her frontal lobe was climbing out of her cranium.

"Is she dead? Is there an answering machine?"

"Yes, there is a machine. She hasn't returned my calls. I sent her a telegram."

"They still have those?"

"Yes, and she still hasn't responded."

"Call the police." Hockey loosened his tie. He hung his jacket up on the closet and started cleaning up the detritus of Eva's night.

"I called the police, and they said . . ."

"What?"

"They said . . ."

He stood still then. When all was silent and immobile. Eva looked up at him like she was a five-year-old grandmother. Girlish, used up, and out of step. "They said she doesn't want to talk to me."

"Why not?"

"They don't know why."

"Oh my God, Eva. I didn't know Mary could be so abusive. What the hell is going on with her?"

"Well, there's got to be a reason."

Hockey took out his pillbox and started swallowing. "What kind of reason could there be?"

Okay, they were strategizing now, together. She began to feel less insane. "Like if I stole her money to buy drugs."

"Did you?"

"No."

"Eva, I think if you did something so bad that this was an appropriate reaction, you would know what it is. What do you want to do?"

"I phoned all of our friends. Thirty. None of them felt that anything was wrong. No one heard anything bad from Mary. One person remembered a time she had come to dinner at our place three years ago and Mary was mean to me but I didn't notice. But that's all I could find. It doesn't make sense to call her alcoholic, flag-waving, Christian cousins, does it?"

"No. Does she come from a family of drunks?"

"Her father drank himself to death. But she says she got over it. That's not possible, is it?"

"What are you, in denial about everything?"

"No."

They laughed.

"Should I call my mother?"

"No. Are you out of your mind?"

Eva thought for a minute. "Yes."

Hockey tied up the garbage bag and wiped off the desktop. "You can only call your mother if you don't need her."

"What should I do?"

"Cut your losses." He was full steam into puttering, opening windows, making coffee, starting the day. He looked at her. She was a shocked person. "Okay, give me the number."

"I've got to talk to Mary," Eva said. "This is all a big misunderstanding. We don't have anything, but we have each other. That's it. When there is no justice, when there is no family, there is Mary."

Hockey pressed *Redial.*

"Hello?" He winked at Eva. "I got the machine. I can make her pick up." He waited. "Hello? This is the local store calling. You seem to have left some money on the counter . . . Hello? . . . Hold on."

He handed the phone to Eva.

"Why are you doing this?" she asked with all sincerity.

"As opposed to what?" Mary snapped.

"As opposed to saying 'This is what I feel and why. What do you feel?' You know, communicating. Facing the problem, whatever it is. Dealing with it. Trying, together, to resolve it. What is it?" Eva felt everything would be all right.

"You're planning," Mary said, like she was talking to the lamppost. "You have a plan that will help us get to a better place. No more plans. No more help. No more better."

"Why not?"

"Because it makes me unhappy?"

"It does?" Eva said, relieved at having something to work with. "I'm sorry, I didn't know. Now that you're telling me, I can have more awareness."

"I don't want awareness. Awareness is a plan. I just want to *be.*"

"But, Mary, you're not just *being*. You're hurting me, and pretending that you don't care. I don't deserve that. It's not neutral."

"Go ahead, be better than me. That's all you want."

"I don't understand what you mean."

"Fuck off."

Mary hung up.

Eva didn't know what to say or do, what to feel or think. It was so unbelievable, it was like it had never happened. That couldn't possibly have happened, could it? *Click?* She'd heard that little click. What was that? She pressed *Redial.* It rang and rang.

"Mary? Mary? Please pick up the phone . . . Mary?" The machine ran out of time.

"Well," Hockey said, "at least you don't have cancer."

"All eight thousand dollars of my insurance claims have been rejected," Eva mentioned.

"You're kidding." He put Bach cello suites on the CD player. They always seemed to be so apropos. "How did that happen?"

"If only I had bought Oxford Plus instead of Oxford, I would have been partially reimbursed. Dr. Kumar is not in the Oxford Plan, she's only in Oxford Plus."

He broke his protein bar in two and gave her the smaller piece.

"When did you figure that out?"

"After seven hours on hold. I spent the night here, on hold on one line and calling Mary on the other. All eight thousand dollars are on my MasterCard with twenty-five-percent interest."

Hockey sat in his chair and looked at his clean, airy office. Bach in the air, his hair newly and perfectly cut.

"Eva?"

"Yes, dear?"

"Do you think I'm going to live?"

"Yes." She got up and washed her face in the wall sink.

"That's it then," he said. "We're stuck with our pointless loss. Mine was biological, and yours is on purpose."

There was a knock at the door.

Eva looked at him. "Why can't I see Mary's pretty face?"

The person on the other side of the door started banging, desperately. Ringing the bell over and over.

"Hey, hey, open up." It was Thor. Eva turned the lock.

"Oh my God," he said, running in. "Turn on the TV."

# 28

Thor, Hockey, and Eva stared at the TV like it was an oncoming train, or the path to the bottom of the well. They could not take in fully what fate and chance had done to their party of good intentions.

On the set, a live press conference was being broadcast from the front lawn of Van Buren High School. A blonde chick wearing a lot of foundation, a light purple ensemble, and white pumps cooed with authority into a sea of microphones. Her name was Bethany Bliss. She was a thirty-nine-year-old divorcée with two kids of her own and a private cocaine hobby. But Eva, Thor, and Hockey had not yet learned any of this. All they knew was that they were in serious trouble, because Eva and Hockey were responsible for someone else and they could barely take care of themselves. Now the person they were responsible for—David Ziemska, their client—was in hell.

"I, Bethany Bliss, am the attorney for the family of Victor Holder, the deceased seven-year-old who was brutally beaten by his uncle, Stewart Mulcahey. Under adult jurisdiction, the district attorney, Bernard South, has announced this morning that he will seek the death penalty in this case. We, the family, place the blame firmly on the shoulders of the police, courts, and social work agencies of Van Buren Township, who have committed severe malpractice and dereliction of duty in this tragic episode. We place the blame on the shoulders of Lieutenant Kevin Bart, who recruited Stewart into giving evidence under severe emotional duress, and Daniel Wisotscky, CSW, for refusing the state intervention Stewart's parents fervently and repeatedly requested."

Thor sank back into his chair and Eva was stunned. She wanted to think about her own problems, but she felt too guilty. Her problems were nothing compared to Stew's. So her mind was blank. Hockey, however, seemed energized by the absurd turn of events.

"God, Bethany is a genius," he said, chomping on his kelp. "What great TV. Look at that backdrop. Small-town

New Jersey red brick school, white steeple, pseudo-Protestant aesthetic for working-class Catholics."

"What are you talking about?" Eva breathed. "Are you out of your mind?"

"Just look at that big hair on Bethany." He pressed the *Mute* button.

"Hockey, Stew just murdered a little boy."

"And David is going to pay for it." Thor's voice was apocalyptically matter-of-fact.

"It's very smart." Hockey was almost laughing. There was a strange glowing enthusiasm. "Big hair on TV conveys small-town parochialism. This helps the rest of the country's sense of this as a monstrous crime. Homosexual crimes, when committed in sophisticated places, are entirely different than when imposed on a bunch of hicks. Hicks are victims of homosexuals, but they're also aesthetically offensive to straight people in big cities. That's why their teeth have to be Photoshopped."

"Are you for real?"

"What's the matter?"

"You sound like a brief." Eva went over to the phone and pressed *Redial*. Then she left a message on the machine. "We're talking about real people here. It's not a game."

"No, it's true." Hockey was bouncing. "In *Newsweek* they ran a cover photo of some white-trash woman who had seven babies at once, and they Photoshopped her teeth so she would look middle-class."

"She wasn't white trash," Eva said, remembering. "She was just white."

"Poor David and Joe," Thor said. "If only the cops had just left that kid alone."

"Well, you're right about one thing," Hockey said expansively, like Sleeping Beauty waking up to a beautiful day. "We're in deep doo-doo, but we can get out of it. Stew got screwed, that's clear. But the state isn't going to take the blame; our client is, unless we're really strategic. After all, Stew was molested, right? By a man. Our man. All of those state officials they're suing are going to put the blame right back on us."

Thor rolled a cigarette, kept his voice flat. "He's such a kid."

"It's about time you noticed." Hockey laughed again.

"What was so funny?" Thor was talking very slowly.

Eva could see him thinking, trying to come up with a way to help Stew. She knew she should be doing the same, but she didn't know how. They looked at each other. Hockey was oblivious, smiling. Watching the TV.

Eva turned her back on the tempting existence of the telephone and sat down at the computer. "How can we save him?"

"Who?" Hockey tore into his protein bar.

"Stew."

"*Bubelah,*" Hockey said, so carefree he balled up the wrapper and shot it into the wastebasket. "Stew is not our client."

"Okay," Eva said, absolutely lost. "Okay."

# 29

All is lost, because absence is found.

"So you grew up in this room, huh?"

"Yeah," Mary growled, feeling sultry and sleek. "I used to bring girls home when I was in high school."

"How did you seduce *them?*"

Wendy giggled. It was a fun fuck, and Mary could feel the girl's excitement, like she was having one of those life-changing sex experiences. Maybe it was her first one-night stand. Maybe the first one that worked. Wendy was as seasoned a homosexual as a girl her age could be, but Mary was just so much older and so fucking hot. She knew how to show her a really good time.

"I would say 'Take me to the movies and you pay. When we're there, you can touch me any way you want to.' I liked how it was in front of everybody. Those poor girls would sweat."

It was three a.m. Her mother would never wake up. She was dead drunk.

"Wow."

"Hey," Mary said as she absentmindedly touched the girl's nipples. She knew they were sore. "You know the fastest way to get a woman into bed, don't you?"

"I think so. Tell her she's intelligent?"

"Yeah." Mary gave her the point. "And listen. Listening works, too."

They were covered in sweat and cum, every orifice satiated.

"You know," Wendy said shyly. "Some girls spend years trying to find someone they can talk to. I'm not that way. I want to have sex. If it's good, there's always something to say. You're sexy. It's fun talking to you." She looked around the bedroom. Now it was used for storage. "How do you like being home?"

"I like it," Mary said, and knew immediately that it was true. "I'm never going back to New York." She'd torn up her airplane ticket that morning. "I know I have to tell my ex-girlfriend, but I don't want to."

"That's cold."

"Whatever. I don't want to help her . . . What do you do?"

"I'm a cop."

*This little dyke?* "In Del Sol? There can't be much business."

"I'm from Freemont," she said. "Three of us got sent here for a seminar."

The garden chimes sang through the window in the night breeze.

"How do you like Southern California?"

"It's so conservative." Wendy shrugged. "Even the criminals are Republicans. You really need to deal with your girlfriend. Just try."

Every afternoon, Mary sat in her grieving mother's garden in Del Sol, California, watching her mother's bitterness, her arthritic hands, old face, lifeless hair. Delilah's will intact, but motivated only by resentment. There was nothing else, after all. Her daughter had not charmed her and her man was dead. All in Mary's life was revealed to have been a false diversion from her mother's disappointment. Mary's girlfriend, her plays, her wish for professional mercy. None of this was real. Only the disappointment was real.

There was no reason to ever go back to New York. As Mary had buried her mother's lover, served the drinks, washed glasses, sat endlessly, watched the TV, she had had so many revelations, none of which she wished to retain.

Eva's pain. Her struggles, commitments, opinions, beauty, friends, and defeats meant nothing. All they ever did was make Mary feel inadequate, lost in her own failings. If Eva failed, Mary had to sympathize. She didn't want to. There was nothing in it for her. There was no point, because it never stopped. Something new always went wrong, and neither Eva's success nor Eva's failure would erase Mary's failure. So what good was it? It was a time waster. Mary had failed herself, and Eva hadn't done anything to stop it. In fact, she had encouraged her to go down a dead-end street.

If Mary had had a stupendous success, one trumpeted in more than newspapers, it would have to be mentioned on television shows that her mother actually watched. Unavoidably in the right magazines at the dentist's office. If Mary could have bought a huge place and a car with her success, then her open homosexuality would have paid off. But she had failed at that, so disappointment was the result. Her mother—widowed, no-hearted—looked at her like she was a broken blender or a stained shirt.

Eva had never really believed that Mary could be an overnight sensation, so Mary didn't want her anymore. Now this cancer thing was coming up. Just like when the legal clinic was defunded. Just like the fucking baby shower. Just like Hockey having AIDS forever. It was always something. Eva would be upset and want help. Mary would have to worry about her and think about it night and day. Maybe even bedpans. Forget it. No way. There was only one bedpan she'd ever want to clean, and that was the one of her needy, vulnerable, futurely incontinent mother, so that her mother would finally know how important Mary truly was. That she was the difference between shit and propriety.

"You need to try."

"No." Mary brought her face to the girl's breast. Apple-blossom beauty. "Trying is humiliating. It points out that I have something to try. I'd rather just stay here. I mean, no one but Eva even cares. My mother is thrilled. She thinks I finally got away from that dyke."

"Yeah, that's pretty funny."

A Mexican man came every other Saturday and earned five dollars an hour to take care of the block, but no one thought this was wrong. No one her mother came into contact with condemned this. It was natural. There was a freedom in that—just to be white, without other people's histories.

That was the irony here. The women at the checkout counters looked just like Mary. They weren't accented, fucked-over immigrants or candidates for workfare filled with resentment and secret languages, their own exotic makeup tips. If Mary had just stayed home where she belonged and gone to a job, she would have been recognized by everyone around her as worthy. As good enough. Her mother wasn't asking for very much. But because Mary tried to be great and spent all those years with Eva, she didn't have anything now. If Mary had stayed closeted, her silence would have protected her from this punishment, the pain of coming out. It wasn't worth it.

Now she could wait for the lemons to ripen on the tree. She'd shop at the pastel mall, the only colors in this panoply being peach, sea foam green, egg yolk yellow, robin's egg blue, and sand. Drive to the mall, drive to the gay bar. Get in the car and freak out. Out of the car is in public. Prepare each time for the human encounter and then return to the Mazda. In New York, once she left her apartment it was all out in the open. People showed one another everything. Del Sol was more sedate, private and civilized. *Who wants to know? Get over it.*

Other people's problems were not fascinating. Del Sol offered tempered intercourse, moderate weather, and casual but clean attire. The choice was this or back to the New York of dark people who move too quickly, think too quickly, and decide the things that Mary never wanted to decide. The others waited for her to decide, and then they decided and she didn't. They liked the responsibility of deciding. She hated it.

Mary could get a job in Del Sol, or the neighboring town of Mesa, for a pittance. Then every night she'd drive her ten-year-old car into her mother's driveway and sit in the garden behind the house like all the neighbors. The street was deserted with flat beige squares of concrete in front of each garage. All the hidden neighbors were sitting quietly behind their own houses, privately. That's what she wanted—privacy—so no one could see her inadequacies or evaluate them. No one measuring her failure. No competition with people she can't beat. Eva had supported her every step on the way to failure.

The night before, they were watching TV. Mary, her mom, and some friends. Someone on the Jay Leno show had said the word "consequences," and Mary ran into the bathroom, shaking. She hated that word. It was a symptom of false sociality. In New York, when she snapped at someone with that American tang, the way every one of her relatives had always snapped at her, the way her grandfather snapped at her father when they worked together on the Ford line in Michigan, the way her father snapped at her mother when she forgot to stop by the package store. This reflex made New Yorkers cringe. They are so weak—they require low tones, false politeness, and explicit reasons for every critique. If she snapped at them, they called her a bitch. Not a Euro-trash unruly one, but a white trash one, and New Yorkers don't even know what white trash is. They think any non-rich white Protestant is white trash. They're so ignorant that blue collar is sexy to them, only if it's rugged but not if it twangs. White blue collar isn't white trash, so how come they don't know the difference?

*"Be nice,"* Eva would whisper whenever Mary got bristly in public. But it was impossible. Do your job, expect nothing, and mind your own business. Delilah suffers in silence here at the end of the continent, sips vodka. Here people have a few drinks and shut up. New Yorkers drink to get livelier. More ideas, more plans. It never stops. Ideas. Plans. Ideas. Plans. They don't even care if they never come true, but they try to make them come true. Why try if it's not going to happen? They just like

planning, so Mary, too, had learned to hope and plan, to gesture pathetically toward strategy. She mimicked them, imitated them falsely, became a cheaper version of them, one that could never succeed at their tricks. They loved planning and she hated it. There is nothing wrong with working hard just to stay in place.

Wendy kissed her again. She wanted one more round.

"In a minute . . . let's have a smoke."

"Okay, but I only have menthol."

"That's fine."

They lit up a Kool.

"Don't give up on your dreams," Wendy said, sharing the cig. "I've achieved my dreams. About work, I mean."

"How old are you?"

"Twenty-three."

"Yeah, well, it's a little more complicated than that. You're young, and you're very pretty. You'll be okay."

Every day at four Mary walked with her mother, slowly, along the beach. It was so gorgeous. The Pacific Coast, a vacuum of beauty, no way to participate. Not like going to a play in New York, where all evening she'd churn and yearn to jump in, be a part of it. You can't envy the ocean. So no disappointment, no agony of exclusion. There's the sea; you can't do anything about it.

This part of Southern California was the true Aryan Nation. Having blonde hair and blue eyes meant nothing here. No butt of jokes or desire. No one knew what *melanin* even means. The subdivision was populated principally by bicepped Barbie dolls. Even the yoga class she tried was too advanced. The gym hadn't offered introductory courses in years, only Advanced Step 2 and Cardio 4. Mary was tall and slim hipped, lanky, great legs. She could be in shape in no time. Those Jewish, Italian, Puerto Rican bodies can never look that way. They just bulk up. If not, they look false. They look overdone and pretentious, out of place being healthy. Deliberate.

Boogie boarding and jogging and drives to the mall belonged on bodies and faces like Mary's. That's what those activities were for. She never wanted to hear them put down again. Beach culture was not a waste of time. That is what time is for. She wanted a Vietnamese woman to wax her legs, a Mexican to clean the garden, and she didn't want to feel guilty about any of it. Her family had worked for a living since 1670. They were still working. Everyone else made it on their backs. They had built this country. They weren't liberals. Del Sol is a hotbed of social rest. And Mary was tired. She wasn't going anywhere.

Mary got up to get a glass of water. The stars were her stars, and she could hear the ocean. There was a terrible sadness suddenly, and then she drank the water. She got over it.

"Hey," she said, bringing the glass to Wendy's lips. "Have you ever seen a play?"

"Yes, it was good."

"Well then you know that in a play the hero's fate has to be made clear before the curtain comes down. Will he be liberated or condemned? The lovers have to have a confrontation or reunite. But there's a big difference between the way people really act and the way they act in plays. This is real life, so I don't ever have to pick up that phone. You know what I like about Del Sol?" Mary lit another Kool.

"The weather?"

"Yeah, I like the weather. I like to sit in gardens with people who work as clerks, in banks or malls, or in software. To get in bed with a cop. No one needing to be recognized by an authority larger than their family. The women at the checkout counter look just like me. They don't try to pass."

"Pass for what?"

"Middle-class."

"So what are you going to do, get a job cashiering?"

"Maybe."

"You're just mad. Soon you'll call your girlfriend. You're not going to stay here."

"I'm from here," Mary said. "Car culture is my culture. She's not my girlfriend. Whatever."

# 30

"Aw, Hockey, get off it. Jeez." Thor was back on his feet now, trying to regain his charm. "Look what they've done to him."

"The kid is a *murderer*, Thor. He murdered a little boy. And no smoking in my office—I have AIDS."

"He's fifteen." Eva took one of Thor's cigarettes, opened a window, sat on the ledge, and lit it. Immediately she realized that doing so was a passive form of resistance to Hockey's authority, and that scared her.

"So what? I knew better than to murder a little boy when I was fifteen."

"They're charging him as an adult."

"He *is* an adult."

"Then," Eva said, throwing the cigarette out the window after one puff, "how can they charge his lover with child molestation? Either he's a man, who should not be brought under court supervision for having a boyfriend. Or he's a child and should be charged in juvenile court." She went back to her computer.

That was what it boiled down to, after all. The hypocrisy. Eva felt trapped, like Stew. No matter where he turned, he faced a brick wall.

"Stew is a murderer," Hockey said, making notes. "Nothing worse happened to him than what happened to us. In fact, it's easier to be a gay kid now than it was when we were little."

"Are you jealous?"

"No." Hockey seemed unsure for one moment. He put his hands in his pockets. "But nowadays they have clubs and things. Look, Bethany's back."

He turned up the volume on the Headline Highlights, drowning out any further conversation. Relieved, they all shut up and watched the same clip again.

"Look, Hockey," Eva heard herself beg. "Stew went through police, courts, and social workers, and no one did anything about that crazy homophobic family."

"Is that what you're going to argue in court?" He postured theatrically. "Blame the family? You've got to •

be kidding. Plea bargain. Wait, here's a new shot of Bethany."

They watched her cross the lawn, wiggle her ass, and walk over to a kind of normal-looking couple, standing by a normal-looking car.

"What bargain?" Eva said, taking notes; it was time to be systematic. "They're not going to bargain. We've got to go to trial and tell them the truth. Stew's relationship with Dave was the happiest thing in his life. His family didn't want him. He's gay. Other gay people are his family. Stew is our child."

"He's not my child." Hockey was quiet.

She shut up and so did he. They were all silent after that. So silent that the sounds of traffic overwhelmed them. Hockey was now officially different. He had put all his vulnerabilities behind him. He now identified with the strong. Eva could see this.

"Do you want to get Dave a life sentence? Honestly, Eva, they are charging Stew as an adult. This is not a gay rights issue. Gay rights is not about child abuse, nor is it about murdering little boys. It's not about fucking little boys, and it's not about killing little boys."

Eva looked at him and tried to smile, but inside she was furious and trying to think of a plan. Okay, Hockey did not have sympathy for Stew, or if he did, it was not the first thing on his mind. Eva couldn't be mad at him for that. She got up from behind the keyboard and Hockey got up from behind his. They both walked to the center of the room, facing off over Thor, who was deep in thought, chewing on an unlit cigarette. She had to appeal to logic. She didn't have anything more powerful to fall back on.

"Hockey, listen." She knew she couldn't be bigger than him, so she tried begging. "We have to go in there and argue that Stew was pathologized for being a gay kid. They drove him crazy."

"Now *you're* crazy. Stew is not our client."

"Let me ask you something, Hockey."

"Yes, Thor?"

The old man stood up out of his chair like he was doing deep knee bends. Like he did them every morning for forty years while holding two thirty-pound weights. "How old were you the first time you had sex?"

"Twelve."

"How old was the other guy?"

"Nine."

"And the next time?"

"Twelve."

"When was the first time you had sex with an adult man?"

"I was fourteen."

"How old was he?"

"In his twenties?"

"Were you molested?"

"It's not the same thing." Hockey was pissed. "I didn't go out and kill somebody."

"I was sixteen." Eva felt sick, like she had done something wrong. She *had* done something wrong—she had helped Stew trust an untrustworthy man.

"Late bloomer," Thor said with a funny gravity.

"We'll argue double jeopardy." Suddenly Eva knew she wasn't going to get her way. She realized something deep about herself. She didn't know how to fight ruthless people. She didn't know how to fight unfair systems. She didn't know what to do about cruelty. She only knew human complexity and the difference between right and wrong. Stew was a victim. He was driven crazy, and now he was acting crazy. He was just a gay kid, like she had been, and his family and the system treated him like a criminal until he became one. If they had just loved him, everything would have been all right. It was like Mary. She was driven crazy. If she had been able to be herself, she could have been. But the powers that be treated her like someone who doesn't matter, and now she was acting that way.

Hockey wanted to argue in court that Stew was responsible for his actions, in order to get David off the hook. But that was not the truth. Stew was driven to murder. But not by Dave. He was driven to it by people who would never be put on trial. Eva couldn't pretend it was any other way. She loved Mary and she loved Stew. She could understand. She realized that she was not afraid to be uncomfortable.

"It's not your case, Eva. How many times do I have to say that? The kid is gone. We've got to save Dave. If you go in there with a gay rights rap, he'll never see the light of day again. It doesn't matter what happens to Stew. David is our client, and David can't go to trial. I'm going to plea bargain and that's that. I wouldn't represent Stew even if I had the chance. He's a murderer."

Eva was quiet, but her mind was churning. *What can I do?* she thought. *What must I do?*

They all smoked that day. Even Hockey, who had once had pneumonia, had a cigarette. The three of them sat in the office puffing and watching CNN. They called in for Chinese takeout, but no one ate it.

Then CNN showed Stew being led to court. It was the first time any of them had seen him. It was really upsetting. Even to Hockey. Stew just looked like a little kid.

"He's so short," Thor said.

"Look at that kid," Hockey said.

Eva stared at him. He was a droopy boy with waist irons and chains on his legs. He was her child. Her.

The camera cut to the on-location reporter interviewing a neighbor in Van Buren Township. Betty Podolsky, a beautician for thirty years who did Mrs. Mulcahey's hair. She had known Stew since he was born.

"I hope he gets raped in prison," she said.

"Tell me one more time," Eva asked. "What are you going to argue in court?"

"That Stew is an adult, thereby consenting to sex with our client, and equally responsible for the act of murder."

"Okay," Eva said. "I'm out."

"Out of what?"

"Out of the case. I'm not going to court to fight for David on grounds that will scapegoat Stew. It's not good for anyone."

"Eva, honey. Listen to me." He said it with pity. "What you want to do will never work. You understand? We are lawyers. We can't do things with other people's lives that aren't going to work. We have to make tough choices."

"I think my way would work."

"I thought you wanted to win," Hockey said. "I thought you wanted to know what it was like to win."

"Not that badly."

"Then," he said softly, "you will never win."

Eva found herself walking down the street with her stuff. She hadn't gone through a process of deciding to leave and saying good-bye. She hadn't laid out all the possibilities and thought through their consequences. She just did it.

She did what Mary would have done.

At the corner she felt scared, regret. But by the time she got to the subway, she had another idea.

*If I don't do what I really think is right, then I am lost. What is the most important thing in my life? What is the one thing I can fight for, no matter what?*

That night when she got home to her empty apartment, Eva wrote a minimum balance check of $250 to MasterCard. Then she cried. She talked out loud to Mary for a while, like she would have if Mary were in the tub. Then she said the word "*Mom?*" She had a cup of tea and dialed Mary's number. It was the machine. She left a message.

"This isn't fair. I love you. If we can talk, everything will be okay."

But there was no response.

# 31

The next day Hockey rode the Amtrak to meet with District Attorney Bernard South. This was his chance to plea bargain for David. Dave had not cried on the phone; he was too doped up by the prison shrinks to respond. The guy was a suicide risk, and Hockey wished they'd just let him do it. Get it over with. But they would rather watch a man squirming on the meat hook. They couldn't let him get off as easily as death unless they were the ones who imposed it. Hockey's own prognosis was quite the opposite: he was being sentenced to life by lethal injection.

He wore his best work suit and set up his notes on the train's plastic folding tray. When he got back he would buy more clothes. Barney's. That was the place to shop. He'd heard the name enough. He'd go in and buy three suits, no matter what they cost. It was a promise. Hockey took out his pill dispenser and swallowed four white tablets, two blue capsules, three orange pills, and emptied some powder into a bottle of Evian. Then he took a red pill and a red capsule and three yellow pills. Then he looked at his notes. These were the treats he had brought with him on the train.

It was clear to Hockey that the protease inhibitors had kicked in again, and he was back at the gym on a regular basis. His arrogance was also back. He was the boss again, and no one was ever going to forget it. Now he was finally angry. Angry that some force had dared to threaten to take his life away, just like it had taken away Jose's. Hockey had always secretly suspected that an early death could never happen to him, and now he was sure. Deep down, as much as he loved and grieved Jose with every breath, he had somewhere considered that Jose was more vulnerable than he was, and that's why Jose died. The train stopped at Hastings.

Jose was so sweet. He had been dead for years now, but Hockey had never put away his clothing, never dismantled Jose's altars or given away his shoes. He still had everything placed in the apartment right where Jose had placed it. He'd never bought anything new. Hockey had thought he was going to die, too, and that this was to have been the entirety of his life. Now, however, he was sure he was not going to die, so he resolved to get rid of Jose's stuff, but he couldn't. There were events that had taken place against these settings, engraved on his body like DNA. They represented his real life, his life with Jose, the only time he had not felt alone. The person who had the decency to stand up for him, to be for him, no matter what anyone would think. How could Hockey ever put that in a box? Then it would end. Forever. And he would be back in the world of strangers. At least Hockey's HIV was the same genetic material as Jose's. The merging of their molecules or paramecia or whatever. It was their child.

The train stopped at Poughkeepsie.

Hockey was alive now, and the person he owed the most to was dead. Nothing. He was not grateful for being alive. No one had handed it to him on a silver platter, life. His lover was dead. For that he was supposed to be grateful? No way.

He was a very lonely man. He wanted to have friends, but it was hard to find the ones who would listen with compassion. Most wanted to tell him how to feel and what to do. Some were so afraid of his suffering that they couldn't bear to know the truth of it. They tried to control what he would say. If he told the truth about how he really felt, they would cut him off. They didn't want to hear it. Some wanted to pretend that nothing bad had happened. "That's all behind us now." Never being uncomfortable was more important than the truth of Hockey's life.

At times he found himself starting to adjust, slightly. Starting to peek into what his life might now be like. And waiting there in his future each time was the lovely face of his sweet Jose. The thought of learning how to live without him was a whole new obstacle. Dying without Jose was hard enough, but living? Hockey wasn't prepared. It meant his worst suffering was before him. It would always be in front of him. It lined the path to his future. His future was strewn with death, fear of death, absence, fear of absence, incredible pain, incredible discomfort, Hickmans, pills, torturous treatments, unpredictable diarrhea, adjusting his fucking medication, side effects, malfunctioning organs, fatigue, emaciation, terrible skin problems, wasting in his face, fat in his gut, rashes, shingles, mollusks that had to be frozen off his cheeks, rashes on his dick, terrible itching skin, so much depression he couldn't get into the bathtub. Today he felt good, except for the diarrhea. But all that pain formed his psyche. The past was his destiny. Why wouldn't anyone else let him say so?

Every night when Hockey came home, he came home to some familiar remnant of Jose. It had all become so codified that those remnants now were Jose. Jose did not exist, so no new evidence that he had ever existed would ever be created. That's why the merest shifting of a shoe destroyed the evidence. It was forensic.

Hockey couldn't wait to take his pills. He loved leaving his office, going to the gym, having sex in the steam room, going home and taking his pills. He loved sitting in the familiar chair in his familiar house, the house where he had spent the best days of his life. The most horrifying. The days that lay before him.

The train arrived at Van Buren, New York.

# 32

Kevin Bart was an enormous, blobby, emotional wreck. He was so suburban, beefy, and emblematic that Hockey could see the bad pop music, and the after-work Jell-O shots. His fear made him that transparent. The rest of the fellows were a bit more upsetting.

There were the two guys from the FBI who never said a word. There was David, pasty and disoriented. He was sweating at the table in his orange prison jumpsuit, hands and waist manacled. He seemed to Hockey like a cinematic child molester. He looked like a child, but he was a man. He had that effeminate pudginess that prison food produced in certain kinds of clients. It made them unsympathetic to others. Stew was also at the table. *So tiny, this kid.* Hockey was surprised at how small and thin he was. A runt. *Too small for his age.* It made David look even more like a child molester, having the two of them there in the room. Then there was Bethany. She had obviously coked up in the bathroom; the blood vessels in her nostrils were flaring. And Stew's parents. Like anyone anywhere. Distressed, uncomprehending, absolutely unequipped to deal with anything complicated or real.

Hockey's job was to blame everything on Bart. Nobody else could handle the responsibility, and Hockey had long ago learned that in court, as in life, you have to blame the person who can shoulder the blame. It makes it easier for others to go along with it. Blame the strong if you can't get the guilty. The justice system is not about justice; it's about order. If punishing the true perpetrator will create disorder, no one will go along with it. Kevin Bart's back was big enough for this burden. He'd get over it. He was young. He could get a second career in real estate.

"We expect you to drop all charges," Hockey said.

"Don't be absurd." That was the judge, Bernard South.

This was a pretrial hearing attended by all parties, where each tried to reframe the paradigm, to restate the terms to their own advantage. Hockey was here to make sure David's case never went to trial. Child molesters don't do well with jury trials, and child molesters of child killers don't do well in front of nervous elected judges and newspaper reporters. He was there to blame the state. Bethany was there to blame David or the state. The state was there to fry two fags, but if they could be satisfied with only one, Hockey's job was to make sure it was the kid, not David, his client.

"Let's face it," Hockey said. "The biggest hole in the state's argument is that you coerced a minor into participating in the prosecution's case against David. A coerced confession is not admissible in the courtroom. No point in pretending that it is."

So far, so good. That was the truth and everyone there knew it.

"Your Honor," Bethany piped up. She had a nice voice. Melodic, an alto, it was comforting. "I expect you to remove criminal charges against my client, Stewart Mulcahey, and remand him to a state mental institution. The boy was molested by a vicious predator, which caused him untold duress. Incarceration would be inappropriate in this case. He needs hospitalization and care."

"Don't be absurd, both of you. I can't drop any of these charges. It's too high profile and you both know it. These two men are going to trial."

The judge was scared. Hockey's job was to make him more scared.

"Excuse me, Judge," Hockey smiled. He was on a roll and feeling great. "Counselor Bliss is right on one point.

David was charged based on a coerced confession obtained by Lieutenant Bart that was not psychiatrically endorsed. Bart is required by law to have the approval of a therapist in such matters, and he did not. That makes the confession invalid, and I think that is obvious to all parties."

"It was my professional judgment," Bart slurped. He was going down fast.

"That Stew could handle the emotional stress?" Bethany was incredulous. She could get work on the soaps. "I don't believe that's your profession, Lieutenant. Especially since Stewart resisted your attempt to install a tracking device."

It looked good. One point for David.

"We have an expert witness." Bethany was giving a great performance. She combined femininity and competence. Played both ways. "He's ready to testify that oftentimes a child, like Stewart, is just not emotionally ready to confront a predator."

Hockey had to nip this one in the bud right away. Especially that word *child.*

"Well, we have an expert witness from the National Center for Protection of Juveniles ready to testify that some teenagers who are engaged in relationships with older men may not share the same values as detectives."

This was his strategy. To neutralize whenever possible, play the middle ground. That was the problem with people like Eva. She was great when someone got their food stamps cut off; then you have to cat-fight. But when your client faces a long jail term, manipulation, deception, and lying were necessary. There was no National Center for the Protection of Juveniles. There was a National Center for the Protection of Children, which had refused to offer an amicus in this case. They don't defend pederasts. But Bernard South didn't need to know that.

"Let me add," Brittany continued, as though Hockey didn't exist, "that the social service department of Van Buren Township exhibited profound incompetence and let down both Stewart and the Mulcahey family, paving the way for this terrible tragedy."

"Completely untrue," warbled the lawyer from the state mental health agency, Gloria Inzunatto. "Everything was determined to be normal. You've read the social worker's report. There was no indication that Stew had any psychological problems. He passed the examination with flying colors."

"Well," Hockey rebounded. "*We*'ve got an expert witness, a psychiatrist, Dr. Miriam Goldberg. She will testify that teenagers engaged in consensual relationships with adults may not share the vindictiveness that intergenerational relationships create in parents and other adults." *Uh-oh,* he'd faltered. He'd repeated that phrase *may not share.* It made him look like he was running out of ammo.

"Let me tell you something right now, Mr. Notkin." South was frothing over that one. "You bring in a gay psychiatrist from New York to testify that it's okay for boys to have sex with pedophiles, and you're going to lose this case. Your client is going away, and I mean no parole."

"Dr. Goldberg is married, Your Honor, and the fact

that Stewart had a relationship with a forty-year-old man shows that he was struggling with his sexual identity."

"That's ridiculous, Counselor." Bethany was laughing on cue. "Stewart cannot legally consent to pedophilia."

She had a big point there, technically.

"By imposing adult sensibilities on a fifteen-year-old," Hockey said, unsure about this one, "the state was inadvertently adding to his difficulties."

"Adults *are* the state," South said. "No compromise."

Bethany blamed. The girl was a real brat. She must have been a cheerleader in high school. "Stew's parents begged the social worker to remove him to juvenile detention, but the state refused."

"It was his professional judgment." Judge South was weakening. Why?

"That Stew could handle the distress?" Hockey was on Bethany's team now. "I don't think so. Stew's relationship with Dave was the happiest thing in his life. His family didn't want him. He's gay. Other gay people are his family." *Goddammit, Eva.* The Mulcaheys didn't flinch. They were comatose.

But Bethany was on top of it. "Blaming the family is not going to get you anywhere. The family has suffered enough because of your client. They have suffered the violation of their son and the death of their beloved grandson. Because of him." Stew's mother started to weep.

"You know it's malpractice," Hockey said. It sounded lame, but actually it was true. That was the only leg he had to stand on, after all. The coerced confession. "The coerced confession is invalid," he repeated. "That is obvious to all parties."

"Nine years," South said, giving in. So that was what he was afraid of: making the cops look bad. "Possibility of parole. Minus time served."

"He'll be out in five years," the FBI guy grumbled.

"Five years too long." Hockey felt good.

"All right, all right, you got your way, Counselor. Lieutenant Bart, remand the prisoner."

David had seemed to be sleeping with his eyes open through the whole volley, but when Bart led him out of his chair, he didn't even look at Hockey, an act Hockey found to be deliberate and contrived. David could have at least been grateful. They all watched, embarrassed, as David stumbled and slowly walked toward the door. Then he stopped, like he'd lost something, and turned toward Stew.

"Save yourself, Stewie," he mumbled weakly. He started to cry, and the guard took him away. A crying pedophile.

It was embarrassing. Everyone was uncomfortable. Stew looked up from his place at the table, in the same prison jumpsuit, same black slippers.

Everyone turned to look at the boy.

"I don't know how," he said back to them.

"Miss Bliss," Bernie South moved on. "Your case is going to trial."

"I want to plead guilty," the boy croaked.

What was this? Hockey stared at Stew. What a nightmare for Bethany. *Shut up, kid,* he was thinking.

He wanted to put his hand over Stew's little cock-sucking mouth.

"Don't be ridiculous," Bethany said, losing it. "That man molested you. You weren't in your right mind."

"I'll never say that." Stew's face was contorted; he hated himself.

*Shut up.* Hockey was screaming inside. Then he said it. "Stop him."

"Stew," his mother leaked. "It's the medication they're giving you. It's messing up your head."

"Don't do this, Stew." That was the father now. A big, lumbering guy. This time he appeared a bit stranger than at the last hearing. Not so normal as before. "You'll get over it. They'll put you in a hospital." He touched his son. "I'm like you." *I'm like you,* he whispered, but Hockey knew he didn't mean gay. It was strangely moving somehow, to see this father try to connect with someone he drove insane. Hockey watched his sincerity. Marty was pleading. It was both tragic and pathetic. Hockey knew what he was seeing, someone who postponed love until it was too late. Here was the result.

Marty whispered to his son, the killer. "Just plead insanity and I'll be the only friend you'll ever need."

"Your Honor . . . ," Bethany said, stalling.

"I'm guilty," Stew said. "I don't know why this happened. It just did. I am the worst of all. That's why."

"This is too much," South said. "I'm going to send this prisoner back to the holding cell. Counselor, get your house in order and we'll reconvene tomorrow."

"Yes, thank you, Your Honor." She wanted to kill.

The judge stood and left them behind. Then the guard picked up Stew by the arm and pulled the shuffling boy out of the office.

"I'm not a bad man," Marty Mulcahey said to no one in particular. "I didn't know what to do. I did my best. You can't control your children. They make their own decisions. I talked to him. I went to see the counselor. I asked him to lay off. He decided not to. All we wanted to do was watch TV, talk to the kids on the phone every now and then. They'd come over once in a while, get married, take care of themselves. Nothing serious."

"Don't blame yourself," Brigid Mulcahey said.

"He's not blaming himself." Hockey watched himself talk. "In fact, he's taking no responsibility whatsoever."

"Shut up," Brigid said.

Hockey looked at Bethany. She was a cold bitch.

"Whatever happens, Mrs. Mulcahey," Hockey said. "You'll never be as bad as Stew. It doesn't matter what you do. Now you can blame Stew. You don't have to blame yourself."

Brigid's eyes glazed over and she looked away. She was not going to engage that. "Everyone's life is ruined," she said. And then she felt better.

# 33

Eva didn't know what to pack. She'd ordered the wrong ticket and had gone to the wrong airport. She'd worn the wrong shirt.

Everything was in place to make a bad impression, but she knew, really, that it didn't matter. Whatever trip Mary was on, it was so deep that Eva's charisma wasn't a factor. But she had to try. She couldn't just watch and wait.

How could Eva have ever considered refusing to try?

It was the worst decision she had ever made in her life. It was the most meaningless. She should have gotten on the plane that first day.

Mary wasn't some girlfriend like "my apartment, my girlfriend, my job." Mary was the love of her life. When Mary walked into the room, Eva smiled. She was always happy to see her, even if Mary was being horrible. *Relationship* wasn't even the right word. It was demeaning. Nothing else mattered. When she imagined living without Mary, she imagined nothing.

Eva stumbled out of the excessively long flight. Two changes, in Chicago and Denver. Then she rented one of those white rental cars. Eva tried to drive, but she really didn't know how. She had gotten a license a couple of years back, but had not had much chance to practice. And the roads were so confusing here. There were no signs and no cross streets. There was no one walking along whom she could ask about directions, and there was no store or anything to pull into and ask the lady behind the counter.

It was all one great whoosh of drivers in the know. All the others already understood exactly where they were going and how to get there. They were beyond needing street signs, and the exits came up so fast, Eva didn't have time to get into the right lane. This wasn't a shtick on her part. This was real. She got caught in the tangle and couldn't get out of it, until she ended up in some place called Encinitas. That wasn't Del Sol. Finally she saw a 7-Eleven and got directions.

"Back onto the highway," the cashier said. She looked like Mary.

Eva bought a piece of red licorice and some cigarettes and stood in front of the 7-Eleven watching the cars zoom by. Anything was possible. Love creates worlds, that's the truth. She knew what she and Mary had between them was far more precious than all else she had ever seen or could imagine. That had to stand for something.

Eva smoked a cigarette and watched the cars. How weird—there was nothing else to look at. No people. Then she threw out the pack. No more cigarettes, no more licorice. She went back inside and bought water. It was a small bottle, a nice fit in her hand. She could get used to anything. Eva got back in the car and pulled out to the freeway.

Love creates worlds.

Right now Mary didn't have faith, but Eva had enough for two. Eva was not afraid of the person Mary was becoming. She loved her, so she could understand. Eva believed in Mary. She knew Mary could do it.

As she drove along, Eva saw the ocean out of the corner of her eye, and then suddenly she came upon it, some kind of coastal road. It was gorgeous, sucking up her anxiety. She'd come to see her true love, Mary. How could she fail? Everyone needs someone to believe in, and Eva believed in her.

This was Southern California. Soon she'd be a health nut. She'd drink Calistoga and take classes in competitive yoga.

No plans, no cigarettes, no causes, no hope.

Just Mary and the beach and a lush backyard.

# Author's Note

Dear Reader,

The novel you hold in your hand was ready for publication in 1999. It reflects a world of perceptions and values firmly grounded in that year. I am very disappointed that neither you nor I had the opportunity to experience each other through this novel in the historic moment in which it was meant to be read.

Prior to writing *The Child,* I published seven novels and two nonfiction books between 1984 and 1998. Why was *this* book so suddenly unacceptable?

There are people who believe that we live in a merit-based publishing environment. For them, the reason I could not find publication was because *The Child* is less deserving than every novel that has been published in the last eight years. And that, therefore, it objectively deserved to remain unavailable to readers.

I, however, have always believed that individual experience is dynamic with its social context.

First, many editors' letters explicitly pointed to the relationship between Stew and David as the reason for rejection. What troubled the editors was my point of view. I did not come out "against" the relationship. Instead I was, as Patricia Powell says in her blurb for this edition, "objective." There is art about what could be, what should be, but there is also art about what is. I feel that the individual discomfort of particular editors about this sexual content, *was dynamic,* with a national trend towards a narrowing of the range of ideas that can be expressed in public. The two Bush presidencies were met by a dumbing down of discourse in mainstream media. There were many times when I felt that I could not hear truthful or complex ideas in public. I could only hear them in private. Economic realities like the mergers of publishing venues, resonate negatively with the trend towards fewer ideas. I experience *The Child* as the place where my lifelong project of expanding representation crashed into the country's shrinking space for new discourse.

Second, the relationship between Stew and David was written against the story of a lesbian lawyer, her lover, and her legal partner. I have written widely about the ways and reasons that lesbian literature is disrespected in America, and I do not have the opportunity to fully replicate that information here. However, I do think it is fair to say that modern lesbian literature made cultural inroads as a consequence of the feminist and lesbian movements of the 1970s and '80s. The cultural conservatism of the 1990s and one of its expressions: niche marketing (see my book *Stagestruck: Theater, AIDS, and the Marketing of Gay America*, Duke University Press, 1998) was a containing reaction to that expansive trend.

In this current environment, many of America's best and most respected editors have never published a lesbian novel. The most successful lesbian writers are either closeted or don't have lesbian content. As a writing teacher, I encounter many young women who are deliberately not writing lesbian content because of the chilling effect of the industry's indifference and neglect. MFA faculties are often not equipped to offer lesbian writers the same kinds of knowledgeable support that straight or gay male work can receive. Writers developing outside of an institutional framework, as I did, no longer have community-based events like Outwrite or Lesbian Writers Conferences to help them develop. Niche marketing continues to keep lesbian literature from being considered an integrated part of American letters. Today, the best-selling lesbian writers in America are British imports. An examination of gay book award nomination lists reveals that best presses in this country have shown a frightening, extremely dramatic decline in their publication of lesbian novels over the last fifteen years.

What makes the fragility of lesbian content *dynamic* with the narrowing of public discourse is that publishing lesbian literature means representing Points of View that are unknown. In a conservative time, most books, films, television shows re-create perspectives that are already known. The familiarity itself becomes the sign of "quality." In an expansive era, the introduction of new ways of thinking is what is praised as "good." But, in our day, the "new" is so rare and unsettling that many people think it is "wrong." And Point of View, not Story, is the most politically charged question in American arts. *How* a moment is perceived and experienced by the character, her right to be the authorial center of her own universe, is what is at question.

I believe that these are the reasons that the publication of this book was so obstructed.

Now for the thank-yous:

I feel enormous gratitude to you, the readers. Twenty-three years after the appearance of my first novel in 1984, rarely a week passes that I do not receive a letter, phone call, email, or personal comment that something I have written has been meaningful in someone else's life. This knowledge gives me strength. Thank you so much, readers, for that precious engagement.

In this period (1999–2007), after fifteen years of work in avant-garde theater (1979–1994), I transitioned to writing for mainstream theater, and began to have plays developed and produced by supportive individuals including Tim Sanford at Playwrights Horizons, Robert Blacker and Philip Himberg and The Sundance Theater Lab, Shirley Fishman and Des McAnuff at The La Jolla Playhouse, and Seth Gordon at The Cleveland Playhouse. I am very grateful to these institutions and individuals for their support. In 2002 I received a Guggenheim Fellowship in Playwrighting, which gave me the recognition that I needed to find the strength to keep fighting for the right of authentic lesbian representation to be part of American intellectual life. I have received lifelong support from The MacDowell Colony. In fact I am writing this note at MacDowell, in the very studio where, twenty-one years ago, I wrote my third novel, *After Delores*. I am very thankful to The Corporation at Yaddo, for their sustained support. And to the Puffin Foundation, and The Paul Anderson Foundation, which provided me with a Stonewall Award, thanks to the support of Kate Clinton. I am deeply grateful to these foundations and the corrective that they provide to industrial gatekeepers.

I never stopped working as an active participant citizen, most directly in my more-than-twenty-year collaboration with Jim Hubbard. Just as the doors were closing on lesbian fiction, Jim and I embarked on The Act Up Oral History Project (www.actuporal-history.org). Thank you Jim for your friendship, understanding, and commitment.

Thank you to Meg Wolitzer.

In 2004, I ran into my friend Diamanda Galas, the great composer and performer, at a coffee place in our shared neighborhood. I told her that I had been struggling for many years to publish a highly engaged novel, and I explained the content and point of view and why they made the book unacceptable. Diamanda told me that she was going to phone a gay male friend of hers who was an editor and tell him—as she memorably put it—"Treat this sister with respect."

This is how Don Weise, of Carroll and Graf, came to this novel and decided to publish it. Thank you Don and thank you so much, Diamanda.

Thank you Mona.

Gratitude to all my true friends, and you know who you are, especially: KT, Julie, Leslie, Jack and Peter, Nuar, Claudia and John and my godchild Ula, Jackie, Gina, Bina, Rabih, Allison and Amy, Heidi, (Uncle) Bob, Erica and Simon, Kevin and Dodie, my cousins: Marcia, Amotz, Gala, Alon, and Ori, my pals at work, my neighbors, Patrick, Dudley, Jessica, Tayari, Mardi, Michael, Michael and Steve, Rachel, Alex, Roz, Larry and Scott, Annie, Ronnie, Patty and Cynthia, Yehudit and Tal, Linda and Jana, Gaelle, Genevieve, Susan, Audrey, Alix, Adrian, My darling the late John Belusso. Thank you for being accountable and for keeping your promises.

—Sarah Schulman
March 2007